Tyler told himself he should drop his hold on Rosa's arm, yet he couldn't bring himself to lose the contact.

Her skin was warm and soft and her nearness made him feel like a man again. A man strong enough to love and protect a woman.

He eased his hand onto her shoulder. The moment his fingers pressed into her bare skin, her face twisted around to his, her lips parted and Tyler's heartbeat quickened.

"There are other ways for a man and woman to learn about each other besides talking," he murmured.

"Mr. Pickens, I—"

"It's Tyler to you." Lowering his voice, he added, "Ty, if you'd like."

Her dark eyes widened just a fraction as they settled on his mouth. "Ty."

The whisper of his name was all that passed her lips before he decided to cover them with a kiss.

Dear Reader,

When my hero Tyler Pickens first appeared on the scene, he was the neighboring rancher no one really knew but everyone speculated about. Some called him a hothead, others labeled him a recluse, and the more people talked about him, the more I wanted to find out for myself just what sort of man had built a flourishing ranch in the rugged New Mexico mountains. Was he really that arrogant and difficult or simply trying to hide a broken heart?

Every now and then good things rise out of the bad. And mistakes, as hard as they are to admit to, are often a springboard to a better, happier place. I hope you will take another trip with me to Lincoln County to see how love can truly rise from a pile of ashes.

Thank you so much for reading my Men of the West stories. I hope each trail you ride is filled with love and happiness.

God bless,

Stella

THE DEPUTY GETS HER MAN

STELLA BAGWELL

ISBN-13: 978-0-373-65747-6

THE DEPUTY GETS HER MAN

This edition published by arrangement with Harlequin Books S.A.

For questions and comments about the quality of this book, please contact us at CustomerService@Harlequin.com.

Printed in U.S.A.

Books by Stella Bagwell

Harlequin Special Edition

†*Daddy's Double Duty* #2121
†*His Medicine Woman* #2141
†*Christmas with the Mustang Man* #2159
†*His Texas Baby* #2199
†*The Doctor's Calling* #2213
†*A Daddy for Dillon* #2260

Silhouette Special Edition

†*From Here to Texas* #1700
†*Taming a Dark Horse* #1709
†*A South Texas Christmas* #1789
†*The Rancher's Request* #1802
†*The Best Catch in Texas* #1814
†*Having the Cowboy's Baby* #1828
Paging Dr. Right #1843
†*Her Texas Lawman* #1911
†*Hitched to the Horseman* #1923
†*The Christmas She Always Wanted* #1935
†*Cowboy to the Rescue* #1947
A Texan on Her Doorstep #1959
†*Lone Star Daddy* #1985
†*Branded with His Baby* #2018
†*The Deputy's Lost and Found* #2039
†*His Texas Wildflower* #2104

Silhouette Books

The Fortunes of Texas
The Heiress and the Sheriff

Maitland Maternity
Just for Christmas

A Bouquet of Babies
*"Baby on Her Doorstep"

Midnight Clear
*"Twins under the Tree"

Going to the Chapel
"The Bride's Big Adventure"

*Twins on the Doorstep
†Men of the West

Other titles by this author available in ebook format.

STELLA BAGWELL

has written more than seventy novels for Harlequin. She credits her loyal readers and hopes her stories have brightened their lives in some small way.

A cowgirl through and through, she loves to watch old Westerns, and has recently learned how to rope a steer. Her days begin and end helping her husband care for a beloved herd of horses on their little ranch located on the south Texas coast. When she's not ropin' and ridin', you'll find her at her desk, creating her next tale of love.

The couple have a son, who is a high school math teacher and athletic coach. Stella loves to hear from readers and invites them to contact her at stellabagwell@gmail.com.

To Marie Ferrarella, who inspired me long before she became my dear friend. Love and thanks. Always.

Chapter One

The sudden sound of footsteps had Rosalinda Lightfoot turning to see Tyler Pickens stepping onto the porch. At least, she figured the tall, imposing figure of a man had to be the owner of the Pine Ridge Ranch. He certainly looked the part. Dressed in jeans and boots and a cream-colored shirt, she figured him to be somewhere in his thirties. Black hair was combed straight back from a darkly tanned face while the expression on his lean features was nothing but grim.

Quickly rising to her feet, Rosalinda placed her coffee on a table next to her lawn chair. As she extended her hand in greeting, she felt a shiver rush down her spine and her pulse leap into a rapid thud.

She spoke first. "Good morning, Mr. Pickens."

For one awkward moment she thought he was going to ignore her outstretched hand, but then he wrapped his big fingers tightly around hers and she was acutely aware of warm, abrasive skin and tempered strength.

"Deputy Lightfoot," he said. "I was expecting a man."

She met his gaze head-on and the coolness of his green eyes was like sliding across an icy pond that could break through at any given moment. Interviewing this man was definitely going to be a challenge, she thought. But being a deputy for the Lincoln County Sheriff's Department made it a part of her job.

"Sorry to disappoint you," she replied.

Releasing her hand, he gestured to the seat she'd just vacated. "Sit," he insisted.

While she followed his suggestion, he pulled up a matching chair and positioned it so that he was facing her.

As she furtively watched him settle back and cross his boots at the ankles, the relaxed language of his body surprised her. She'd expected to find a tense, rigid man ready to explode at any moment. Perhaps the rumors she'd heard about the man were exaggerated or wrong. Or maybe his moods were always changing. In any case, there was something about him that made it impossible for her to tear her gaze away. He'd not expected her to be a woman. Well, she'd certainly not expected him to look so tough and masculine.

Sharp cheekbones angled beneath his hooded eyes, while a thin, aquiline nose led down to a pair of rough-hewn lips. He was the epitome of man, sex and whipcord strength, and for the first time in a long, long time Rosalinda felt the woman in her staring with interest.

Sipping the coffee that Gib, the house servant, had kindly served her, she gave herself a mental shake. The lack of sleep last night must have left her punch-drunk. Normally, she never looked at a man the way she was looking at Tyler Pickens now.

Clearing her throat, she said, "I'll try to make this quick, Mr. Pickens. I understand you're busy dealing with the mess the fire left behind."

"Ah, yes," he said softly, "the fire. The reason for your little visit. I don't suppose you have any information on how it started."

"Not yet," she said briskly. Before she'd made the trek out here, Undersheriff Brady Donovan had briefed her on all he knew about Tyler Pickens. During that meeting she'd learned he was a single man and had been ever since he'd moved to this ranch over nine years ago. No one had heard or seen family visiting and the only friends he seemed to have were his ranch hands. And Laramie Jones, the foreman of the Chaparral Ranch and Tyler's neighbor to the south, had a somewhat amiable relationship with him.

He grimaced. "I should have known better than to ask that question. You probably wouldn't tell me even if you had a long list of suspects or motives."

"Probably not," she said, softening her reply with a faint smile. As best as she could gauge, last night's fire had stopped at the river, which was situated no more than three miles from the Pine Ridge ranch house. The brunt of the flames had spread mostly over the Chaparral Ranch, the Cantrells' land, blackening and scorching acres and acres of forest and meadowlands. Thankfully, Laramie Jones and his crew had saved the Chaparral livestock by working through the night to move the cattle as far away from the fire as possible. As for Tyler Pickens, he'd not reported any cattle dead or missing.

"So what do you expect to get out of me?" he asked. "I can't do your job for you."

Trying her best not to bristle at his cocky attitude, she purposely delayed answering as she took another leisurely sip of coffee. Maybe he didn't have friends or family around him because they found him too difficult to deal with, she thought. Or maybe the fire had left him in a testy state of mind.

"I'm glad you realize it's not your job to play lawman. Arson is a serious matter." Lowering her cup to her thigh, she noticed he was looking at her keenly now, as though seeing a woman with a weapon strapped to her hip was an oddity or completely distasteful to him. The idea had her lifting her chin and calling upon the confidence that Sheriff Hamilton had tried to instill in her. He'd often called her a good deputy. She had to believe the good sheriff. Moreover, she had to believe in herself.

His green eyes narrowed. "So the fire chief has ruled the incident as arson?"

"Accelerants were used." She wasn't going to elaborate on the evidence. To do so might compromise the case, especially when she didn't yet know whether this man was involved.

"That's hardly a surprise." Faint sarcasm tinged his words. "There wasn't a lightning strike within a hundred miles of here last night."

She wondered if anyone had ever tried to slap that smirk from his face. It certainly wouldn't be an easy feat to accomplish, she decided. The man was a picture of toughness.

"Other things can cause fires, Mr. Pickens. Like cigarettes, campfires, burning trash, welding sparks—just to name a few. Were any of your men working in the area yesterday where the fire started?"

His black brows formed a straight line across his forehead. "Why the hell are you questioning me about my men? The Cantrells are the ones you should be interrogating!"

His defensive attitude didn't surprise Rosalinda. From what she'd learned, this past year the adjoining Chaparral Ranch had been plagued with all sorts of problems. Some of which had spilled over onto the Pine Ridge Ranch. And Tyler Pickens hadn't been bashful about voicing his displeasure over the matter. But that could be a guise, she told herself. He could be pretending to be a victim when in actuality he was the instigator. But why would this man want to cause trouble for the Cantrells? And did he really seem the criminal type?

But Dale's ex-girlfriend never seemed like a psycho, she reminded herself. On the outside, Monique had resembled a shy, soft-spoken librarian with hardly the gumption to say boo to a mouse. But she'd been an obsessed woman with evil intent on her mind. *She fooled the hell out of you and your boyfriend. You need to remember that appearances can lead you in a dangerous direction.*

Shoving aside the cold little voice in her head, she said, "Deputy Harrigan is currently at the Chaparral Ranch interrogating folks there."

The subtle flare of his nostrils told her that he was struggling to keep a rein on his temper. But in all fairness, the man had every right to be aggravated. He'd had a portion of his land burned to a crisp and now he was being interrogated by the law. Under those conditions, no normal person would be in a happy mood.

A sneer lifted one corner of his lips. "So they sent you up here to dig into my ranch and my personal business."

Her backbone straightened to a rigid line. "I'm hoping that *digging* won't be necessary, Mr. Pickens. I expect you'll want to help in this investigation, to volunteer anything and everything that might help us discover who committed this devastating crime."

Long, tense seconds ticked by as his cool gaze slipped over her face, her khaki shirt, then on to the long line of her legs. In spite of the fact that many women were working in law enforcement these days, they were still sometimes subjected to nasty slurs and sexual insults. But the look in Tyler Pickens's eyes said he wasn't dismissing her as a deputy sheriff, he was seeing her as a woman. And that unsettled her far more than his brash attitude.

"How long have you worked for Sheriff Hamilton?" he asked.

This was her interview, not his. Still, she didn't want to

make him so angry that he clammed up. Like it or not, she needed this man's cooperation.

"Long enough," she answered evasively. She wasn't about to tell him she'd only worked as a Lincoln County deputy for eight months. He'd think she was too inexperienced. He couldn't know that prior to becoming a deputy sheriff, she'd already worked a year and a half for the Ruidoso Police Department. And since becoming a deputy she and her partner had already busted a major theft ring, helped capture two fugitives and recovered stolen livestock.

His gaze settled on her left hand. "You have a family, Ms. Lightfoot?"

Why would he be asking her something that personal? she wondered. It was none of his business. "Deputy Lightfoot," she corrected him. "And no. Do you?" she countered.

Even though his gaze slipped from hers, she could tell by the tight corners of his mouth that he didn't appreciate her question. Why? Was he estranged from his family?

"No," he answered. "Except for my cook, Gib Easton, I live here alone."

"Hmm. Must get lonely," she mused aloud. "Lonely enough to want to create a little excitement by setting a fire?"

His response was a deep, rich laugh that had Rosalinda staring at him in wonder. The dimples in his hollow cheeks, the gleam of white teeth against his dark skin was so endearing she found herself smiling along with him.

"You find that funny?" she finally asked.

"Very." Rising to his feet, he walked over to the edge of the concrete porch and with one hand made a sweeping gesture toward the mountain range to the right of them, the narrow valley directly below and in the far distance, the glint of a river winding its way southward. "All of this is mine, Deputy Lightfoot. I've worked hard to make it into the ranch it is today. I get excitement from watching a calf born or a foal running at its mother's side. Not from flames eating up my precious grazing land."

He made perfect sense. Draining the last of her coffee, she placed the cup and saucer aside and walked over to where Tyler Pickens stood next to an arched column of rock that supported the porch roof.

If she were to get really close to the man, she thought, the top of her head would do well to reach the middle of his chest. A fact that had nothing to do with the matter at hand, she quickly reminded herself, so why was she thinking it? After the long, nightmarish ordeal she'd been through with Dale, she'd not wanted to be close to a man again. Neither physically nor emotionally. But something about this rugged rancher was making her forget the heartache and fear that she'd endured.

Clearing her throat, she tried her best to focus on her job. "How long have you owned this ranch?" she asked, even though county records had already told her.

He glanced at her. "Nearly ten years."

Beyond the manicured lawn shaded by huge Ponderosa pines, the ground sloped away to a green valley floor, where the working ranch yard was located. From her angle, she could see a maze of barns, sheds and corrals. Cowboys on horseback were moving cattle from pen to pen, while others pitched hay and spread feed into mangers and troughs. Cows bawled and a horse's loud whinny was answered by its nearby pal. It was a beautiful June morning in southern New Mexico, the kind that could almost make a person forget that something bad had happened the night before.

Keeping her voice brisk, she said, "I understand you asked Quint Cantrell to sell a stretch of Chaparral land to you and he refused."

"That's right. A couple of years ago, I approached him about buying a piece of land that runs adjacent to my property. Most of it is grazing land, something I need more of. Neither he nor his grandfather wanted to part with it."

"Did that make you angry?"

He looked utterly bored. And perhaps he did consider her questions stupid, but to her it was legitimate.

"Disappointed, Deputy Lightfoot. Not angry. I'm still hoping that someday they'll have a change of heart. In the meantime, I don't want their land burned or any other mishap to happen to their ranch. I happen to like the family."

"But you are aware that the Chaparral Ranch has been experiencing some problems."

"That's a damned fool remark! You bet your ass I'm aware of it! I run purebred Herefords up here. I don't want any of their Angus bulls over here breeding my cows! I don't want my fences cut or my cattle straying off their home range! I'm sick of Cantrell problems turning into mine!"

His icy eyes were now spitting fire, making it clear to Rosalinda that he was a passionate man.

"I can appreciate that," she told him.

"Somehow I doubt that." As quickly as it flared, the anger disappeared from his face. "The Cantrells are an old, established family around here. They're known and loved by a lot of folks. I'm still considered a Texan, an interloper. Nobody gives a damn what happens on the the Pine Ridge Ranch."

She turned a thoughtful gaze toward the busy ranch yard. "Frankie Cantrell, Quint's mother, is from Texas. In fact, she's back there now visiting her older sons. Did you know that?"

"Is that question a part of your investigation?"

"No. Just my curiosity."

A disapproving groove appeared between his brows, and Rosalinda got the impression he wasn't used to having personal questions directed at him. And suddenly she was wondering about far more than his feelings toward the Cantrells or their adjoining land. This ranch was even more remote than the Chaparral and he'd already admitted that he lived here alone. Outside of raising cattle and horses, what did he do for companionship?

Apparently deciding she was simply talking as one person to another, he said, "Yes, we're both from Texas. Back there I lived on my parents' ranch, the Rocking P, just west of Austin. But Mrs. Cantrell said she'd lived in the southeast, in Goliad County, and we'd never met before I moved here."

"What made you want to come to New Mexico?"

"To make a place of my own. And I like this area."

"It's a far distance from Austin," she stated the obvious.

"That's one of the reasons I like it," he said flatly.

Which could only mean he'd left something behind there, Rosalinda decided. The same way she'd left a part of her life behind in Gallop. But none of that had anything to do with the present.

"Well, concerning the fire, Mr. Pickens, do you have any reason to think one, or more, of your hands might have set the blaze?"

Expecting him to lash out again, he surprised her by shrugging. "All my men have been with me for several years now. They're good, dependable guys."

Folding his arms against his chest, he turned toward her and Rosalinda's gaze was drawn to the fabric stretched across his biceps, the cuffs rolled against his corded forearms. "Don't get me wrong, Deputy Lightfoot. There've been squabbles among my hands. Throw ten men together for eight, ten, twelve hours a day and eventually there'll be friction. But nothing serious between them and the Chaparral hands."

"Do you know if any of them are buddies with Chaparral hands?"

"Not that I'm aware of. You'd have to ask them."

She nodded. “Well, I would like to speak with your men. Ask them a few questions,” she told him.

“If you want to talk with Gib, you’ll find him in the kitchen. The rest you should find down there.” He jerked his head in the direction of the ranch yard. “But I wouldn’t expect any confessions,” he added wryly.

She shot him a cool smile. “I’m not expecting confessions, Mr. Pickens. I’m looking for pieces of information that will tell me the comings and goings of your men prior to the fire.”

She drew a card from her jeans pocket and handed it to him. “Here’s my name and a sheriff’s department number where you can reach me. If you think of anything that might be helpful in this matter, don’t hesitate to call.”

He took the card and without looking at it, stuffed the piece of paper into the pocket on his shirt. “I’ll do that.”

Extending her hand to him, she said, “Thank you, Mr. Pickens. I, or someone with the department, will keep you informed.”

“I would appreciate that,” he said.

He took her hand again, only this time he didn’t shake it, he simply held it. Heat swam beneath the surface of her cheeks, and Rosalinda felt a strange current pulling her toward the rancher.

Disturbed by the sensation, Rosalinda withdrew her hand and stepped off the ground-level porch. As she strode to her truck, she felt his gaze following her, but she didn’t look back to confirm her feelings. For now, she’d seen enough of Tyler Pickens.

Chapter Two

Back on the porch, Tyler picked up the deputy's empty cup and entered the house. In the kitchen he found Gib cleaning up the aftermath of their breakfast.

Upon hearing Tyler's footsteps, the older man, who possessed a head full of snow-white hair and a brown, leathery face, glanced over his shoulder to study him with faded blue eyes. "That was short and sweet."

Short? Tyler felt as though his time on the porch with Ms. Lightfoot had stretched into hours instead of a few minutes. As for the sweet, he couldn't deny the deputy had caught his attention. Not with her words, but with her looks.

He didn't know what the hell had just happened to him. He wasn't interested in women in that way. Not since DeeDee. She'd torn a hole right down the center of his dreams, his hopes and everything he'd planned for his future. She'd driven a wedge between him and his family and ripped his world apart in the process. Because of DeeDee, the thought of any woman these past ten years had chilled him. Yet something about Rosalinda Lightfoot had snared every masculine cell in his body and had him staring at her like a damned fool.

"She didn't have that many questions." He dropped the cup into a sink of sudsy water. "I tried to tell her she's wasting her time questioning me and my men."

Gib walked over to a round wooden table and gathered up a handful of condiments. "Is she?"

His mind still swirling with the image of the woman's long, dark hair, chocolate-brown eyes and soft pink lips, Tyler looked at his longtime friend and employee.

"Are you implying that one of us is an arsonist?"

The crevices around Gib's mouth curved downward toward his chin. "Sometimes people are good at hiding things about themselves."

Gib Easton had once worked on the Rocking P for Tyler's father, Warren, but when Tyler had decided to make the move to New Mexico, the man had chosen to accompany him here to this mountain ranch. Gib had been one of the few people who'd clearly seen that Warren Pickens played favorites with his twin sons and that Tyler had always ended up with the short straw. He'd always been grateful for Gib's support. Now their years together had made Gib the one man Tyler could completely trust.

"That's true," Tyler admitted. "But I have faith in my men."

"Art and Joey were riding fence in that area yesterday. Sawyer told me that much."

"Think about it, Gib. Can you picture those two carrying jugs of gasoline on their horses? Not likely."

The older man cocked a curious brow at him. "Gas was used to start the fire?"

Clearly annoyed with himself for letting a woman rattle him, Tyler muttered, "Damn it, I don't know. Deputy Lightfoot said some sort of accelerant was used. I just assumed it was gasoline."

Gib crossed the room and shoved the salt and pepper shakers onto a cabinet shelf. "What else did she say?"

Pausing at the table, Tyler glanced out the glass patio doors situated a few steps away. From this angle, he could see the deputy's truck parked near the main barn, but she wasn't anywhere in sight. Nor were any of his ranch hands. She probably had them gathered in the barn. Or maybe she was cagey enough to talk to each of them independently. Either way, Tyler could imagine how the men would react to her. She was as sexy as hell. The kind of woman that made a man think of long, pleasurable nights.

"She wanted to know if I was angry enough at Quint Cantrell to want to burn his land."

Comical confusion wrinkled the older man's features. "Where did she get that idea? Quint is a friend. At least, he's always appeared to be friendly."

"Because Quint wouldn't sell me that tract of land near the river she thinks I might have wanted revenge."

Gib shook his head. "Why, that was more than two years ago. Took you a damned long time to retaliate."

Tyler sighed. "It's her job to ask questions. She's down at the ranch yard now with the men."

"And you didn't go with her?" Gib was clearly aghast. "Those guys will eat her up."

"I wasn't invited. Besides, I have a feeling Deputy Lightfoot can handle herself." And if he got wind that even one man was rude to her, he'd personally punch him out. He wouldn't tolerate his men behaving in any way less than respectable.

"I hope you're right," Gib replied.

Tyler walked over to a corner of the room and after plucking his cowboy hat from a hall tree, he levered the gray felt onto his head. "I have to go to town, so I won't be here for lunch."

Gib's voice followed him as he strode to the door. "You know what people think of you, Ty. They think you're trouble."

Tyler's jaw tightened. Yeah, he was trouble, he thought bitterly. All he'd ever done in his life was try to walk the straight and narrow, to do the right thing no matter what it cost. And it had cost him one hell of a lot.

"I don't give a damn what people think," Tyler muttered.

"Not here. But back in Texas..."

"Was a lifetime ago, Gib. That doesn't matter." He paused at the open doorway long enough to cast the cook a pointed look. "If you're worried my reputation is going to get you in trouble, you don't have to hang around and wait for the axe to fall. You going back to the Rocking P would give Dad one more reason to gloat."

"Gloat, hell! Warren Pickens will never see this old man again. Dead or alive." The older man shoved his hands into the soapy water and began to scrub a plate. "My home is here with you. Is that settled?"

This was the perfect time to tell Gib just how grateful he was for his unwavering loyalty, Tyler thought. But he'd never learned to actually form the sentiments in his heart into words. He'd always believed in letting his actions speak for his feelings. While his twin brother had been exactly the opposite. He'd had a gift of gab and affectionate phrases had rolled off his tongue like molasses off a hot biscuit. And they'd meant little more.

"It's settled," Tyler said, then moved to the older man and clasped his shoulder briefly. "I'll be back by midafternoon."

Minutes later, Tyler was driving through a section of road where flames had eaten grass and underbrush right up to the edge of the bar ditch. Slowing the truck, he stared with disgust at the soot-covered ground, the charred tree trunks. The person responsible needed to be choked to within an inch of his life, just to show him how the wildlife felt when they were being consumed with smoke and running for their lives.

But he wasn't going to hold out much hope that the sheriff's department would find the culprit. Unless they'd found plenty of worthwhile clues at the origin of the fire. And if that had been the case, Deputy Lightfoot hadn't let on. No, she'd been wasting time with useless questions about his feelings toward the Cantrells.

Trying not to think about Rosalinda Lightfoot, he pressed down on the accelerator. After rounding a sharp bend in the road, he spotted a Chaparral truck parked at the edge of the narrow dirt path. Seeing Laramie Jones sitting beneath the steering wheel, Tyler pulled alongside the vehicle and stopped. As he rolled down his window, Laramie did the same.

"Out surveying the damage?" Tyler asked the dark-haired cowboy. Laramie had been the foreman of the huge neighboring ranch for far longer than Tyler had lived in New Mexico.

He shot Tyler a weary grin. "Could've been worse."

"Amen to that. You lose any cattle?"

"No," Laramie answered. "What about yourself?"

"One cow cut her leg, that's all," Tyler told him. "She must have spooked and bolted through the fence. Thankfully, most of the herd was up on a higher range last night."

"That's good," Laramie replied.

Was the other man thinking how convenient that sounded? Tyler wondered. Was Laramie part of the group that considered him to be nothing but trouble? He didn't want to think so. Laramie Jones was one of the few men who had befriended him since he'd moved here.

I don't give a damn what people think.

Tyler's outburst to Gib a few minutes ago hadn't been completely true, he thought. He didn't mind if people considered him cocky, or hot-tempered or a weird recluse. Those were trivial and sometimes even accurate descriptions of him. But the idea that anyone might consider him a criminal was another matter completely.

"A deputy is up at the ranch right now questioning my men." Pulling off his dark aviator glasses, he looked directly at the foreman. "If any of them had anything to do with this, Laramie, I want them to be severely punished."

"I have no doubts about that. A couple of deputies are at our place, too. Let's hope they get to the bottom of this. And quick."

Tyler released a heavy breath. "So how is Quint taking all this? Last night when we were moving cattle I didn't see him around."

"He's angry and worried. That's how he's taking it. His wife, Maura, is pregnant and last night she was so upset over the fire that I convinced him to stay with her and let the rest of us men handle the cattle."

From what Tyler understood, the baby was going to be Quint's third child, coming after two young sons. In all honesty, Tyler had to admit he was envious of the man. At one time in his life he'd wanted children desperately. More than anything, he'd wanted to be a father and raise his children far from the stranglehold Warren Pickens had placed upon him. But DeeDee hadn't wanted to be a mother. Hell, after less than a year of being married, she'd not even wanted to be his wife. She'd wanted to have fun and enjoy herself. And Tyler's twin, Trent, had been more than eager and willing to show her a good time.

Now, nearly ten years later, Tyler fought to forget how he'd bent over backward to please his young but fickle wife. In the end, she'd not been worth his efforts and all his trying had made him look like an even bigger fool. Especially with his father continually taunting him with warnings that Trent was the man DeeDee really loved. And as it turned out, Warren's stinging predictions had come true. In the end, DeeDee had divorced him and married Trent. Not only that, the two of them had moved in to the very house that Tyler had originally built for himself and his wife.

Hell, what was he doing thinking about DeeDee or Trent at a time like this? Tyler wondered, as he gave himself a mental shake. He didn't give a damn about either one of them. They deserved each other.

Putting the truck into gear, he said, "Well, you and Quint have my number. If either of you need me for anything, just call."

"Thanks."

Tyler lifted a hand in farewell and put the truck into motion. A quarter of a mile down the road, his cell phone rang and seeing the caller was his foreman, he quickly answered. "Yeah, Sawyer?"

"Sorry to bother you, Ty. But you'd better get back here to the ranch. Quick."

Tyler bit back a sigh of frustration. Sawyer was a competent man. He didn't annoy Tyler with trivial problems, so clearly something had to be wrong. "What the hell has happened now?"

"It's that deputy. Seems as though Santo didn't take too kindly to some of her questions. He blew his stack and told her he'd taken feed sacks, a jug of kerosene and a cigarette lighter down to the property line and set the fire. Said he'd wanted to burn every damned Cantrell to a crisp! Now she's about to haul him to jail!"

Muttering a curse under his breath, he promptly jammed on the brakes and wheeled the truck around in the middle of the road. "Stall her if you can! I'll be right there."

When Tyler reached the ranch yard he instantly spotted

Santo standing at the front of the deputy's vehicle with his hands cuffed behind his back. Sawyer and two other cowboys were standing several yards away, anxiously watching the scene unfold. Instead of worrying that his men might cross the line with the pretty deputy, Tyler realized he should've been more concerned about her taking advantage of his men.

After braking the truck to a jarring halt, Tyler leaped to the ground. He trotted over to where Deputy Lightfoot was speaking on a two-way radio affixed to the dashboard of her truck.

He waited until she leaned across the seat to hang the mike back on its holder before lashing out at her. "What the hell do you think you're doing?"

Slowly turning from the vehicle, she fastened a look of warning on him. "That should be clear to you. I'm taking your employee into custody."

Tyler would be the first to turn over any man on this ranch if he was guilty. But the only thing Santo would set a match to was a candle when he said a prayer. "That's stupid! Santo hasn't done anything!"

Her lips pressed tightly together as her dark brown eyes leveled a pointed look at him and at that moment the odd thought of kissing her shot through his mind. What would it feel like to pry those lips of hers apart and feel the soft skin of her cheek pressed against his?

Her voice suddenly interrupted his wandering thoughts. "Mr. Pickens, I suggest you let the law do its job. Otherwise, you might find yourself in a pair of handcuffs."

He didn't know whether to burst out laughing or curse. "If you haul Santo to jail, you'll be making a huge mistake."

"Your man just confessed to the crime," she retorted. "I'd be stupid not to arrest him."

"You insulted him. He said all of that out of spite because he's angry!"

Stepping forward, she wrapped a hand against the back of Tyler's arm and urged him several feet away from the vehicle and out of the earshot of Santo and the other men. Tyler was acutely aware of the warm weight of her hand, the flowery scent wafting to his nostrils.

"Mr. Pickens," she said lowly. "When I left your house less than an hour ago, you implied you had no qualms about me interrogating your men. Now here you are interfering. Maybe you should start explaining yourself."

It suddenly dawned on Tyler that if their roles were reversed, he wouldn't be showing the calm patience that she was projecting at the moment. The insight was enough to dissolve his anger and make him even more aware of her touch and the deep, dark depth of her eyes.

"Okay, I'm guilty of interfering. I'm sorry. But in this case I think you need to know what's going on here."

Dropping her hand away from his arm, she rested her hands on her hips. "Hmm. Well, exactly what is going on here?"

"Santo couldn't have started the fire. Yesterday I sent him over to Roswell to pick up a horse. He didn't return until late in the evening and when the fire started, Santo and I were both down at the stables dealing with the new horse." He inclined his head to a point beyond her shoulder, where a long barn with a wide roof protecting the whole length of the building, which stabled more than two dozen horses. "We'd barely gotten the horse unloaded and into its stall when we started to smell smoke."

She stared back at him as she weighed the sincerity of his words. Then, finally, she inclined her head toward Santo. "I'll talk to him again. You come with me. But don't say a word. Understand?"

"Santo will hear a few choice words from me," he assured her. "But that will be later."

Seeming to accept his promise, she motioned for him to join her and they quickly returned to where his chief wrangler stood passively waiting for the deputy to haul him away.

A man in his sixties, Santo had worked for Tyler for eight years and since his wife had died several months ago, he'd moved into the bunkhouse and lived on the ranch full-time. Tyler understood the man was going through a tough emotional patch. Otherwise, he would have fired him for pulling such a stunt with Deputy Lightfoot.

She said to Santo, "I think you'd better tell me your story again, Mr. Garza. It's not adding up to your boss's account of your activities yesterday."

Remorseful now, the man looked at her, then Tyler. "Okay. I was gone to Roswell. I didn't set no fire," he mumbled.

Her eyes rolled with utter frustration. "You stated that you wanted to burn every Cantrell to a crisp. If you didn't set the fire, what was that about?"

"I added that for good measure," the wrangler explained. "Miss Deputy, don't you know when someone is feeding you a line of bullsh—uh—manure?"

She shot Tyler an exasperated look. "Evidently your man doesn't understand he can get into deep trouble by lying to a law official. I could take him in, you know. For giving false statements, impeding an investigation and—"

"But you won't," Tyler interrupted. "Because you and I both know that Sheriff Hamilton doesn't have time to deal with this sort of nonsense."

"Neither do I," she snapped.

Turning to Santo, she gave him a stern upbraiding before finally releasing him from the handcuffs. The horse wrangler didn't press his luck by hanging around or tossing any more sarcastic jabs at the deputy, especially in front of his boss. Instead, he quickly headed in the direction of the stables with the other three ranch hands close behind him.

Lifting his hat from his head, Tyler raked a hand through his thick hair and heaved out a weary breath. This morning was hardly going as planned. "I'm sorry about this, Deputy Lightfoot. Santo is—well, he's an independent cuss. He sometimes has the idea that rules are for other people to follow, not him. Believe me, I'll get the message over to him."

"That might be a good idea. Before he gets himself into a serious situation."

She walked around the truck to where the driver's door still stood ajar. Within the cab, he could hear the dispatcher relaying information to another officer and Tyler suddenly wondered if Deputy Lightfoot had already alerted the sheriff that she was making an arrest regarding the fire. He hoped not. It would hardly shed a positive light on her ability to judge people and the situation.

Whether she makes a fool of herself or not is hardly your business, Tyler. If she takes a fall for mishandling the investigation, it's not your worry.

Even though the pestering voice in his head was giving him good advice, he pushed the annoying noise aside. For some reason he didn't understand, he wanted this woman to succeed. And not just because it would be to his advantage to have the arsonist found and punished. No, this was a personal feeling. Something he'd been short on for a long, long while.

"Are you finished interviewing the men?" he asked.

"For now." She climbed into the truck, shut the door, then looked out at him through the open window.

Amazed by the crazy pull she had on him, he couldn't stop himself from stepping closer to the truck door. "I'd like to thank you again, Deputy Lightfoot, for being so understanding about Santo. His wife died a few months ago and he's been struggling to get back to normal. If not for that, I would fire him. As it is—"

"Forget it," she cut in briskly. Then, turning her focus back inside the truck, she started the engine.

"I'd rather buy your dinner," he said, unable to stop the rush of words from tumbling out of him. "Just to show my gratitude."

That jerked her head around, and Tyler could see shock arching her black brows and widening her dark brown eyes.

"Sorry. It's against department policy to accept gratuities," she said stiffly.

"Okay. Is it against department policy for deputies to eat dinner?"

A grimace tightened her lips. "No. We do get to eat from time to time."

"Then would it be a crime for someone to sit down at your table and eat at the same time you were eating?"

She stared at him. "No. But you paying for it would be."

He grinned and was totally amazed at the spurt of excitement skittering along his veins.

"Well, *Deputy* Lightfoot, you know how things sometimes go at busy restaurants. Meal tickets get mixed up. One diner's order might get added to someone else's. It's all just innocent confusion."

He could see the corners of her mouth twitch, making it clear that she was trying her best not to smile. The idea pleased him far more than it should have.

"You know, Mr. Pickens, right now you're proving to me that you'd make a perfect criminal."

He chuckled. "Perfect, huh? I'll take that as a compliment."

She let out an exasperated breath; then, after a few moments of mulling over the idea, she said, "All right. It just so happens that tonight I'll be having a meal at the Blue Mesa. If you just so happen to stop by about eight o'clock, I'll be sitting there in a booth."

"Eight o'clock!" he exclaimed. "That late?"

"I'm working a split shift today. Some of us don't get to hang up our spurs after the sun goes down, Mr. Pickens."

Casting her a suggestive smile, he said, "Sometimes I wear mine all night, Rosalinda."

"Deputy Lightfoot to you, Mr. Pickens."

Before he could make a reply to that, the window slid upward and he could do nothing more but watch as she reversed the truck away from the barn, then drove away.

The dust of her vehicle had barely dissipated with the wind when a voice sounded directly behind him.

"What the hell was that?"

Turning, Tyler saw that Gib had walked up behind him. Apparently, the cook had noticed something going on here at the ranch yard and had walked down to check things out for himself.

"That was the deputy leaving," Tyler told him.

"I'm not talking about the deputy. I meant you laughing. What was that all about? I can't see anything amusing about part of the ranch going up in smoke and the law snooping all over the place."

It was about him flirting and actually getting a charge out of the whole exchange between himself and the sexy deputy, Tyler could have told him. But Gib didn't need to know that; especially since it had been a momentary thing. He didn't want the older man worrying that he was going to get himself involved in another painful position with a woman. Because that was the last thing Tyler would ever do again.

"Oh. I'm just feeling good, I guess."

Frowning, Gib said, "You sure as hell weren't feeling good when you left to go to town a while ago."

"That was before I saw parts of the burn in daylight. Made me realize how lucky I was to only lose one hay meadow and no cows."

Gib thoughtfully stroked a thumb and forefinger against

his chin. "That's so. But she—that deputy—was about to haul Santo off to jail. I thought you'd be upset with her."

"No need for that. She came around to my way of thinking."

Gib studied him for another moment and then, with a puzzled shake of his head, replied, "I'm going to the house."

The cook had taken only a few strides in the direction of the sprawling hacienda when Tyler called out to him. "Don't bother making supper for me tonight. I'll be eating in Ruidoso."

Halting in his tracks, Gib glanced over his shoulder. "You'll be eating supper in Ruidoso, too? Why?"

"I've got a date. That's why."

Turning, Tyler walked to his truck to leave the flabbergasted cook staring after him.

Chapter Three

"Rosa, you look so pretty tonight!" Loretta, a longtime Blue Mesa waitress, stepped back from the booth and gave Rosalinda a full-length inspection. "I can't ever remember seeing you in a skirt. Must be something special going on."

Loretta's remark brought a sting of heat to Rosalinda's face. She'd donned the turquoise tank top and white tiered skirt because it was a warm summer evening. Not because there was anything special about tonight, other than the idea that Tyler Pickens might walk through the door and sit across from her.

Ever since she'd driven from the Pine Ridge Ranch this morning, she'd been asking herself exactly what she was doing. Cozying up to the enemy or simply wanting to be a woman again? No matter which way she answered, it would be wrong. Outside of an official interview, she had no business conversing in any form or fashion with Tyler Pickens. And why would she want to? He wasn't the most charming or sociable guy she'd met in the past few years, though he was probably the sexiest. He was also a mystery. One that she wanted to unravel.

"Nothing special, Loretta. I do wear skirts and dresses, you just always happen to see me whenever I'm working."

The young woman with a long red ponytail pulled out her order pad. "That's for sure. You're always working. Especially at this time of night."

"I worked overtime last night investigating the fire out on the Chaparral Ranch. So I got off early this evening."

Loretta tapped the end of her pencil against her chin. "Oh, yeah, I heard about the fire. Have you caught the person who set it?"

She gave the waitress a sidelong glance. "How did you know that someone set it? It could've been a wildfire."

Loretta chuckled. "Rosa, you know how word gets around. Lawmen are in here for breakfast, lunch and dinner. Besides, if it had been a simple wildfire you wouldn't have been working overtime."

"You're a smart girl," Rosalinda said wryly. "What are you doing wasting away here in this restaurant?"

A furtive look came over the waitress's face. "Waiting for a man to walk through that door and sweep me off my aching feet."

She might as well keep waiting, Rosalinda could've told her. Gallant knights didn't ride up to restaurants and save damsels in distress. A few years ago Rosalinda had worked as a waitress, too, at the Brown Bear Cantina, a dingy little diner down on the Mescalero Apache Reservation. During that time she'd fallen in love with a regular customer, but her feelings had all been one-sided. Johnny Chino had loved someone else and was now happily married to the woman. Thankfully, he'd never really guessed her flirting meant anything serious. Otherwise, it would be awkward working as his fellow deputy now.

"Good luck," Rosalinda told her.

A customer at another table called out to Loretta and she said to Rosalinda, "I'd better go check on that table. I'll get your coffee on the way back."

The waitress swished away from the corner booth and because she was nervous, Rosalinda picked up the menu that Loretta had left behind. The Blue Mesa wasn't a fancy place. But the simple, home-cooked food was so good that patrons ignored the scruffy seating and worn tile. The old establishment had been a focal point on Mechem Drive for more than five decades, and during all those years the city police and county law officers had used it as a gathering place.

Moments later, Loretta returned with her coffee and as Rosalinda stirred a huge dollop of half-and-half into the cup, she heard the bell over the front door jingle.

Glancing up, her heart immediately gave a hard jerk as she watched Tyler Pickens emerge from a small entryway at the front of the room. Except for replacing the cream-colored shirt with a pale blue one, he was wearing the same cowboy gear he'd worn this morning. And like it had this morning, the sight of him struck her hard.

He paused at the entryway long enough to allow his gaze to sweep the room. When it finally landed on her, he acknowledged the recognition by a faint incline of his head, then quickly made his way through the busy eating place until he reached the far back wall where she was sitting.

"Hello, Mr. Pickens," she greeted him.

"What a surprise to find you here, *Ms.* Lightfoot." The wry slant to his lips made the glint in his eye seem even more suggestive. "Quite a coincidence, isn't it?"

Because she didn't know whether to groan or laugh, she ended up doing neither. And since she was off duty at the moment, it hardly seemed appropriate to remind him once again that she was Deputy Lightfoot to him, not a Miss or Ms.

She said, "Ridiculous is more like it."

He took a seat on the opposite side of the table and eased off his gray hat. As he placed the headgear next to him on the bench seat, her gaze traveled over his black hair. It was thick with a slight wave bending the ends. Her mother would say the man needed a haircut. The wayward strands curving around his ears and onto the back of his neck gave him a reckless, bad-boy look. Add that to the day-old growth of beard shadowing his jaws and chin and the image was downright lethal, she decided.

He looked across the table at her. "Why? Because you told me where you'd be? Or because I'm here?"

"Both."

"You're out of uniform," he stated the obvious as his gaze swept over her. "I got the impression you'd be stopping by here on your work break."

"Since I worked through most of the night last night, another deputy offered to take over my shift. Once I leave here, I'm going to go home and crash."

"Well, you look very pretty."

From everything Undersheriff Donovan had told her about Tyler Pickens, she'd not expected him to be a flirt or anything close to it. Apparently, the man had a side to him that others hadn't seen before. So why was he showing it to her?

Deciding she might not want to know the answer to that question, she picked up her coffee cup and gazed into the brown liquid. "Thanks."

He was about to make some sort of reply when Loretta arrived. As the young woman took their orders, Rosalinda could see the waitress was bursting with curiosity, but thankfully she didn't ask to be introduced.

Once she'd left, Tyler picked up the glass of ice water that

Loretta had served him and took a hefty drink. Rosalinda was momentarily distracted by the long, brown fingers wrapped around the slender glass. This morning as he'd clasped her hands, she'd been struck by his calloused skin, the roughness that told her he used his hands for more productive things than signing paychecks.

"Do you live here in Ruidoso?" he asked.

"At Ruidoso Downs," she answered. "I used to live down on the res, but that made the drive to Carrizozo even longer. In case you didn't know, that's where the sheriff's department, courthouse and county jail are located."

"I know where it is," he told her. "But this is a huge county. If you arrest someone in the Ruidoso area do you have to drive them all the way to Carrizozo to lock them up?"

Shaking her head, she said, "No. We can use the local lockup here as a preliminary holding cell. Then later we transport the suspect to the county jail. And you're right about this county being huge. The sheriff's department has jurisdiction over 4,859 square miles. That's why Sheriff Hamilton likes for his deputies to live all over the county. Makes it easier for us to keep up with what's going on in our area and to better deal with local problems."

"I see."

He rested his shoulders against the back of the padded seat, and Rosalinda was drawn to their width and the slow, sensual movements of his body. The man was more than enough to take a woman's breath away. So why wasn't he married? Or at the very least, playing the field? She could only presume he wasn't interested in having a relationship with a woman. And yet there were moments he looked at her with something like hunger in his eyes. Not necessarily for her, but for something that was missing in his life. The whole notion unsettled her.

"So you lived down on the reservation," he remarked. "Are you Native American?"

"Half. My dad is from the Zuni tribe and my mom is white. They have a little farm south of Gallop—near the river."

"Hmm. How did you end up all the way down here?"

"How did you?" she countered.

A clever smile lifted the corners of his lips, and Rosalinda was suddenly wondering what it would feel like to be kissed by this man. It had been so long since she'd had a man's lips pressed to hers, she wasn't sure how her body would react. Maybe her mind would freeze everything inside of her and she wouldn't be able to feel a thing. Or maybe she'd want to run and never stop running.

Oh, God, why was she thinking these things now? Tyler Pickens wasn't here as her date! He wasn't here because he found her attractive, intriguing or anything else. He was simply showing his gratitude for not hauling his wrangler to jail.

"All right," he conceded, "I ended up here because I didn't like where I was."

"Hmm. I don't believe I've ever heard that come out of a Texan's mouth."

His lips twitched with sour humor. "It was the circumstances, not the place, that pushed me to move here."

"Ah, yes, circumstances," she repeated softly. "We all have them, don't we?"

"Some more than others," he said.

Rosalinda felt something inside pushing and prodding her to confide in him, to relate exactly why she'd come to this southern part of the state. The realization startled her. No one, except for Sheriff Hamilton and Undersheriff Donovan, knew about her past and the traumatic experience she'd been through. She'd never really wanted anyone to know about the strange and dangerous situation she'd gotten herself swept up in. But the moment this man had set his cool green eyes on hers, she'd felt a connection. The guarded walls inside her had started trembling and cracking. It was the most reckless feeling she'd ever experienced in her life.

Clearing her throat, she sipped her coffee and told her heart there was no reason for it to bump along at such a high speed. Until last night, when Brady Donovan had briefed her, she'd not even known Tyler Pickens existed. She wasn't going to confess her personal life to this man, she promised herself. She wasn't going to do anything with him, except eat a meal.

"So how is Mr. Garza?" she asked. "Still angry with me?"

"Since this morning, I've not talked to him. I'll give him a chance to lick his wounded ego before I light into him. As for being angry with you, Santo isn't the sort to simmer and carry a grudge." It was a trait that Tyler admired and wished he could apply to himself. But try as he might he'd never been able to forgive his family for hurting and ostracizing him. *And why should that matter?* he glumly asked himself. Neither his twin brother nor father needed or wanted his forgiveness.

Hell, it had been over nine years since he'd spoken directly to either of them. That's how much they cared. As for his sister, Connie, she'd always avoided controversies in the family just so she wouldn't have to face Warren Pickens's wrath. And Edie, his mother, had tried to stand up for him, but her opinion had never held much weight for a man who didn't respect women. Now his mother was the only one who still loved him enough stay in touch. Even though her calls and letters were few and far between.

"Well, I thank you for explaining about his wife. It makes me feel a bit better to know it wasn't entirely me that made him fly off the handle." Shaking her head with self-recrimination, she said, "I should have realized what he was doing. But to be honest, I'm still green at my job. Sheriff Hamilton says it takes years of experience and learning to catch all the nuances needed to make a great lawman. It's clear that I have a ways to go."

One of his brows arched upward. "Does he know what happened this morning with you and Santo?"

She tried to laugh, but the sound came out more like a strangled cough. "Of course he knows. Everyone in the department heard me call in the arrest. I'll be the butt of their jokes for months."

"I wouldn't let that bother me. People have talked about me for years and it hasn't killed me yet."

His green eyes appeared to soften, and Rosalinda found herself drawn into their depths. Whenever he looked at her it was like he understood she'd been to hell and back, that she had her secrets just like he had his. Perhaps that was why she kept getting the urge to tell him private things about herself.

Glancing furtively at him, she asked, "You think people around here gossip about you?"

Before she could answer, Loretta arrived with their food. She placed a Reuben sandwich in front of Rosalinda and served Tyler a chicken-fried streak smothered in gravy. After the waitress had refilled their drinks and left the table, Tyler answered Rosalinda's question.

"I know for a fact they gossip about me. Once my foreman was asked if I was an extremist and kept my house stockpiled with rifles and weapons."

Frowning, Rosalinda picked up her sandwich. "Do you have a stockpile of weapons?"

His chuckle conveyed how ridiculous he considered the idea. "The only weapon I possess is a hunting rifle and I keep it locked away because I quit hunting years ago. I think—well, when people don't know about something or someone, it sparks their imagination and they start making up things." He sprinkled pepper over his food and reached for his fork. "And I suppose I make matters worse because I don't mix and mingle with the folks around here."

"Why don't you mix and mingle?"

He shrugged. "I don't dislike people, Ms. Lightfoot, but integrating into the community is for other folks. Not me. If someone wants to be my friend, that's good. But I don't go out searching for them."

What about searching for women? she wanted to ask, but stopped the words before they could pop from her mouth. The last thing she wanted was to give Tyler Pickens the idea that she was interested in him in a personal way.

What kind of idea do you think you're giving him by inviting him to meet you here tonight? You are interested in him, Rosa. You just don't want to admit it.

Kicking back the incriminating voice in her head, she turned another question on him. "What about the folks back in Texas? Do you still keep in touch with them?"

His gaze quickly dropped to his food and several awkward moments passed before he eventually answered, "No. That part of my life is over."

There was a tone of finality to his voice that spoke of loss and pain. The sound sent questions about him and his family spinning through her mind. "Oh. So you've lost your parents?"

Looking up, he cast her an empty smile. "No. They're quite alive and well."

That stunned her and she suddenly realized he was like a mystery box wrapped in layers and layers of richly textured paper. She wanted to peel them away, to peek inside at this rancher, who was unlike any man she'd ever met. But that wasn't a part of her job. Not when her motives for the questions were completely personal.

After forcing down several bites of sandwich, she said, "There are times I really miss my family. I have three brothers and one sister, but I don't see them or my parents very often. I rarely get enough free time to make the trip up to Gallop."

"Then why don't you live up there? Near them?"

Because the pleasure of being in her old hometown had been ruined by a man and the obsessed woman who'd refused to relinquish her hold on him.

"I like it better down here," she told him flatly. "My job—the people—it's all home to me now."

His eyes narrowed as his gaze swept a perceptive path over her face, and Rosalinda felt her cheeks warming, her breaths coming just a bit faster. Could he actually see the haunting memories on her face? Even more, could he see exactly how much he was affecting her?

"When you say home, I take it you don't share it with anyone. A husband or boyfriend?"

His question filled her with a sense of fear. Which was ridiculous. Since her ordeal with Dale, she'd not written men totally out of her life. She wanted to be normal. She wanted to be loved. And yet the idea of being intimate with a man again was like venturing a walk through a bear-infested forest. Even though Dale had been a gentle, loving man, he'd been carrying problems that she'd not known about. Problems that had eventually exploded onto her. And the more she'd tried to stand by her man, the more dangerous everything had gotten.

"I'm single and unattached," she finally answered. "But I'm only twenty-six. I'll have plenty of time later on to think about marriage."

Across the booth from her, Tyler tried to focus on his food, but it was hard to do when the pull of the sexy deputy kept urging his gaze back to her side of the table. She wasn't married or living with a boyfriend. The fact had him smiling inside.

Damn it! He must have breathed in too much smoke last night. Something had clearly messed up his thinking. Otherwise, he would have never suggested meeting this woman for dinner. True, he was grateful that she'd not caused real trouble for Santo, but he could've shown his appreciation in some other way. Like a simple thank you.

But she'd sparked something in him that had shaken him out of a long, cold sleep. He'd not been able to resist the urge to spend more time with her and let her warmness thaw him back to life.

"You're very young," he commented. "How long have you worked in law enforcement?"

"I worked for the Ruidoso Police Department for a year and a half before I applied for the job of county deputy. I've worked for Sheriff Hamilton for about seven or eight months now."

"Hmm. How did you decide you wanted to be a law officer? Was that something you'd always planned to be?"

"No. When I first got out of high school I always had intentions of becoming a schoolteacher. I love children and Mom always said I had a way with my younger brothers." She placed what was left of her sandwich back onto her plate and toyed with the pile of potato chips lying next to it. "But all of those plans got forgotten for a while. And then I became friends with Johnny Chino. Do you know him?"

Tyler rolled the name through his memory bank. "Not personally. I've heard the name. He's some sort of famous tracker, isn't he?"

"Used to be. He's a deputy now. Anyway, he and his wife—she's a medical doctor here in Ruidoso—both urged me to go to police academy. They thought I'd be good at it. And once I started considering their idea, it began to appeal to me. Now I like to think that I'm helping people be safe."

She smiled at him and Tyler felt something inside him go soft and helpless. Her white teeth against her creamy tan skin, the impish curl at the corners of her plush lips was an intoxicating sight. Especially since he rarely received a genuine smile from anyone.

"What's been the most rewarding thing about your job so far?"

"Finding a lost little boy. The mother feared he'd been kidnapped from their front yard. But I have brothers so I understand how adventurous boys can be. So I followed my hunch and found him at the nearest baseball park. He'd climbed down in the dugout and fallen asleep."

"Wow. That must have made you feel like a true heroine," he said.

Her smile turned modest. "I don't know about that. But the look on the mother's face when I handed her son back to her is something I'll never forget. And since then I've had a few more proud moments. Especially when Sheriff Hamilton praised me for busting a local theft ring. But that's enough about me. What about you? What made you decide to be a rancher?" she asked.

"I grew up with horses and cattle."

The smile lingered on her lips. "Well, no one in my family ever worked in law enforcement. But I didn't let that stop me. My family and friends say I'm stubborn, but I like to think of myself as determined."

Since he'd only just met her, he didn't know those things about her. But he did know she was very beautiful. After his divorce, he'd never imagined himself looking at another woman and feeling a strong desire. For the past ten years he'd never been tempted to spend more than five minutes with one. But here he was doing just that.

"I'm sure you're a very good deputy. Sheriff Hamilton wouldn't have any other kind. But don't you ever worry that you might find yourself in a dangerous situation?" he asked.

Something flickered in her eyes just before they dropped to her plate, but the glimpse was too quick to determine what she was thinking or feeling.

"I've been in dangerous situations before and I've learned

how to handle them. As a matter of fact, I teach a self-defense course to women one night a week at the community center. The way I see it, the stronger a woman is both mentally and physically, the safer she'll be."

She was not a petite woman. Her height was probably taller than average and there was nothing fragile about her generous curves. No doubt she would be physically strong. But were her defensive skills enough to wield off a gun or a knife? It was an image he didn't like to contemplate.

DeeDee hadn't been physically strong. She'd been a tiny little thing that thought lifting a hair brush was enough of a morning workout. But mentally, she'd been as wily as a cat. She'd known exactly what buttons to push and what cards to play to get what she wanted. In the beginning her wants had been Tyler. But that had quickly changed once Trent stepped in and began working his charm on her.

"Your family doesn't worry about you having a dangerous job?" he asked.

"My family understands that I don't have to be a deputy to be threatened."

He was trying to figure out that odd statement when a shadow loomed up beside their table and he looked up to see a stocky, auburn-haired man dressed in a deputy's shirt and jeans. He was squinting at the two of them as though he couldn't believe what he was seeing. For some reason, the idea irked Tyler.

"Rosa, is that you in a dress?" he asked incredulously.

The moment she glanced away from Tyler and up to the other man, instant recognition hit her face and she smiled as though she was seeing an old friend.

"Hank! I thought you were off duty tonight, too!"

He shook his head. "I had to go back out to the Chaparral."

She scowled faintly. "Why didn't you let me know? I could have joined you."

The deputy, who appeared to be in his early thirties, shrugged one shoulder. "You needed the rest. And it was a matter I could deal with myself."

She let out a long breath as her eyes darted awkwardly from Hank to Tyler, then back to Hank. "Well, thanks. Mr. Pickens and I just happened to be having supper at the same time tonight and decided to have our meal together," she explained. "Have you two met before?"

"I don't believe so," Tyler said as he glanced to the other man.

"Hank and I usually work as partners," she told him.

Tyler extended his hand to the lawman. "I'm Tyler Pickens. Nice to meet you."

Hank shook his hand. "Deputy Hank Harrigan. Same here," he said. "I think I remember seeing you at the Chaparral several years ago. When the rustling ring was busted."

"You probably did," Tyler replied. "I was there to help hunt for Alexa. Thankfully, Jonas found her before anything terrible happened."

Hank nodded. "Yeah. A real Texas Ranger to the rescue. All of us around here were impressed by him." He glanced over his shoulder to a table across the room, then back to Rosalinda. "Well, I'd better get over to my table. My buddies are waiting. See you in the morning, Rosa. And you take care, Mr. Pickens."

Tyler nodded at Hank's parting words before he turned his attention to Rosalinda. Now that her coworker had left, her expression had become strained.

"What's the matter?" he asked her. "Are you worried about him seeing you having dinner with a suspect?"

"You're not a suspect. Not exactly," she corrected, with a grimace. "I just wish—well, it doesn't matter. Anyway, one way or the other, he would've probably heard about you and me having dinner together."

Tyler put down his fork. "Are you interested in him? I mean romantically?"

She grimaced. "No. But he's sort of interested in me. And I've always put him off by telling him I'm not interested in dating. Now he's going to think I was lying to him."

Tyler glanced across the room to where the deputy had taken a seat at a table with two more law officers. From the corner of his eye, he noticed all three men were glancing surreptitiously in their direction. He didn't know whether to be amused or irritated by the attention.

"Your partner is going to believe we're dating just because we're having a meal together? That's being pretty presumptuous, isn't it?"

She didn't answer immediately and he glanced across the table to see a faint blush had painted her cheeks a soft pink. The color made her features even lovelier.

"I'm sorry. That was silly of me to say. It's just that… well, I don't do this sort of thing for any reason. And Hank knows that." She quickly dabbed her lips with a napkin, then changed the subject completely. "If you're finished, I'd like to leave now."

Clearly, she was flustered. But whether he was the reason for this change in her, or if it was the sudden appearance of Deputy Harrigan, he had no way of knowing. Something Tyler was certain of, though, was that he was far from ready for his time with this woman to end.

"Sure. I'll signal the waitress and we'll get out of here."

Five minutes later, Tyler had settled the bill and the two of them left the restaurant by way of a side door. The exit led onto a large deck where patrons could take their meals outdoors. Since it was dark, only a handful of people were sitting around the wooden tables partaking of drinks.

Beside him, Rosalinda lifted her face skyward and let out

a long sigh. "It's good to be away from prying eyes. Besides, the night is beautiful. It's much nicer out here, anyway."

Not wanting her to make a quick dash to her vehicle, he curled a hand around her elbow. "Let's walk over to the back of the deck and look at the creek," he suggested.

She hesitated, but only for a moment. "All right."

Since the restaurant and adjoining deck were built at the base of a mountain, the property behind it consisted of thick forest. Directly beneath the back side of the deck, a small creek tumbled its way down the hillside toward a larger branch of water. In the light of day, trout could be spotted swimming in the crystal clear stream. Tonight, the only things visible were shiny dapples created by moonbeams slanting through the pine boughs.

As they stood side by side, staring down at the moving water, Tyler told himself he should drop his hold on her arm, yet he couldn't bring himself to lose the contact. Her skin was warm and soft and her nearness made him feel like a man again. A man strong enough to love and protect a woman. It was a sensation he'd believed he would never experience again and it filled him with immense pleasure.

He said, "I'm sorry if my being here tonight will cause you trouble at work."

"It won't. I'll simply explain to Hank that you and I had a few more things we wanted to discuss."

"You mean about the arson? Or each other?"

Her attention on the creek, she let out another long breath. "We're not supposed to be discussing each other."

Releasing his hold on her arm, he eased his hand onto her shoulder. The moment his fingers pressed into her bare skin, her face twisted around to his, her lips parted and Tyler's heartbeat quickened.

"There are other ways for a man and woman to learn about each other besides talking," he murmured.

"Mr. Pickens, I—"

"It's Tyler to you." Lowering his voice, he added, "Ty, if you'd like."

Her dark eyes widened just a fraction as they settled on his mouth. "Ty."

The whisper of his name was all that passed her lips before he decided to cover them with a kiss.

Chapter Four

Time was nonexistent to Tyler as his lips roamed over Rosalinda's. The seconds that were ticking away didn't matter. At least, not to him. All that did matter was the unexpected pleasure warming his blood and making him forget the loneliness of the past years.

But then, just as quickly as he'd started the kiss, she ended it by easing her mouth from his and placing a step between them.

"I have to go," she murmured, her gaze riveted on her feet.

As she turned to leave, Tyler caught her by the upper arm and for one split second he considered jerking her back into his arms and kissing her again. But he quickly squashed the urge. Something told him that Rosalinda was too important to waste on a momentary indulgence.

"All right," he said slowly. "I'll walk you to your vehicle."

With his hand gently curved around her arm, they walked across the wooden deck, then down the steps to where a row of cars were parked along the street curb. Along the way, she remained silent until they reached a black pickup truck with the county sheriff's logo stamped on the side.

"Here's my truck," she told him.

They paused in front of the vehicle and though Tyler knew he should drop his hand and allow her to leave, he couldn't bring himself to let her go.

"I've enjoyed this evening, Rosalinda."

Her gaze fluttered up to his face and even though there was only the streetlamp to illuminate her features, he could see a pained look in her eyes. Had his kiss done that?

"Thank you for dinner, Tyler."

She said his name with easy sweetness and the sound poured through him like warm honey and coated all his rough spots.

"My pleasure."

Her lashes lowered at the same time her tongue came out to moisten her lips. It was all Tyler could do to keep from bending his head and kissing her all over again.

"I'm sorry if I seem a little weird to you," she said with a sudden rush of breath. "But I— Well, kissing is not something I've done in a long, long time."

"Neither have I. I wasn't sure I even remembered how."

Her eyes widened. "What was that? A test just to see if you could?"

Groaning, he bit back a curse word. "Not hardly. That was pure instinct. A beautiful woman standing next to me in the moonlight. I might seem old to you, Rosalinda. But I'm not dead by any means."

"Old?" Her laugh was shaky with nerves. "When I look at you, that's the last thing that comes to my mind."

"Really? What's the first?"

Shaking her head, she reached for the door handle. "That you're a dangerous man."

The urge to pull her into his arms and somehow convince her that she could trust him completely was so strong it gripped him like a sharp pain.

"Looks can be very deceiving, Rosalinda. I hope you'll come to realize that."

"I'll think about that," she said, then pulled open the door. "Good night, Tyler."

Reluctantly, he dropped his hold on her arm and stepped back. As she climbed into the truck cab, a sense of separation washed over him. The feeling not only stunned him, it made him feel like a complete idiot. This woman was practically a stranger and he wasn't about to get tangled up with a rough-and-tumble female who wore a pistol on her hip and a stubborn look in her eyes.

"Good night," he replied.

With the door shut between them, she quickly started the engine and backed out of the parking slot. Tyler didn't watch her drive away; instead, he climbed into his own truck that was parked down the street. But as he drove home to Pine Ridge Ranch, he couldn't help but wonder how soon it would be before he saw Rosalinda Lightfoot again.

The next morning, Rosalinda was sitting at her desk, putting her notes together from the day before, when Hank entered the small office space.

Not bothering to glance up, she greeted him with a cheery good morning.

"Mornin'," he replied.

Swinging her chair around, she watched the stocky, rusty-haired deputy walk straight to the small coffee machine situated on a cluttered table in one corner of the room.

"What's the matter? Late night?" she asked.

"Not very."

With a foam cup of the steaming liquid in his hand, he

turned back to his desk and Rosalinda couldn't help but notice the slump of his shoulders. The fact that he'd continued to work last night, while she'd had the whole evening off, made her feel a little guilty, even though it wasn't her fault.

"You sound tired," she observed.

"I'm okay."

Rosalinda suddenly decided the tone of his voice was more sulky than anything. More than likely, he was brooding because she was out last night enjoying herself while he'd been working. Well, he could just brood. It had been weeks since she'd had a few extra hours off duty. She deserved a break now and then.

Trying to temper the irritation in her voice, she said, "Look, Hank, I didn't ask to be off last night. Vance volunteered to fill in for me and I took him up on the offer. If you have a problem with that, maybe we should talk it over with Brady."

Grimacing, Hank plopped into his seat. The movement caused the coffee to splash over the rim of the cup and onto the thigh of his jean. Cursing, he placed the cup on the desk and directed a glare at her. "I don't have a problem with anything. Except you fraternizing with a suspect!"

So that was it.

Slowly and purposefully, she walked over to Hank's chair and stared down at him. "You have evidence that Tyler Pickens set the fire himself or ordered it set? Or for that matter, do you know for certain he's caused any sort of mischief on the Chaparral Ranch?"

Her questions brought a tinge of color to his cheeks. "No. But—well, it just doesn't look good. You out with a man like him."

There were so many retorts rushing to Rosalinda's tongue that she couldn't manage to spit any of them out. "Drink your coffee," she finally muttered. "You clearly need it."

Turning on her heel, she went back to her desk and tried to focus on her hastily scribbled notes, but the angry steam inside her was fogging her ability to see or think.

After a moment, Hank asked, "What's the matter with you?"

No doubt, her sharpness had taken him by surprise. Since she'd come to work as a county deputy, she and Hank had been the best of buddies, with hardly a strained word between them.

Swiveling her chair so that she was facing him, she said, "You are my working partner, Hank. Not my keeper. Being seen with Tyler Pickens is my personal business."

His face turned a deeper shade of red. "So that little scene with you and him last night at the Blue Mesa was personal?"

She groaned outwardly. "I didn't say that," she shot back at him, before letting out a long breath. "Actually, we agreed to meet to talk a little more about the fire. That's all there was to it."

The mocking twist of his features said he wasn't at all convinced by her explanation. "You needed to put on a skirt for that?"

No matter if she had deliberately dressed up for Tyler's sake, Hank was crossing into private territory. And she wasn't going to be shy about pushing him back to where he belonged.

"What I wear or don't wear is my concern. Not yours or any man's," she said bluntly.

Faint surprise flickered across the deputy's face; then he shrugged and grinned as though he realized just how much he'd ruffled her. "Sorry, Rosa. But you're a rookie. I feel protective of you."

A strained breath eased out of her. "Forget it, Hank. Let's just get to work and see if we can figure out who was playing with matches."

"Right. Between the two of us, we ought to be able to solve this thing and make our bosses happy."

Glad that the awkward tension between them had dissolved, Rosalinda turned back to the paperwork on her desk. "That would put a few feathers in our caps," Rosalinda agreed.

To please her superiors and prove to them that she was a capable deputy with enough determination and grit to get things done would fill her with confidence and pride. But oddly enough the idea of making Tyler happy by finding the culprit felt equally important to her. And that was crazy. Just downright crazy.

She'd only known Tyler Pickens for little more than a day. Yet the man was continuing to consume her thoughts to the point where she could hardly make sense of the statements she'd taken yesterday from the Pine Ridge Ranch hands. Even though hours had passed since their meal and subsequent kiss, she couldn't get any of their time together out of her mind.

From the moment he'd started talking last night, she'd felt herself being drawn to him. The rich textures of his voice and the subtle movements of his body had slowly and surely seduced her and when he'd kissed her, she'd reacted to him like a woman starved for the touch of a man. Dear God, she could only imagine what he'd been thinking about the hungry way she'd responded to him. The only saving grace about the whole ordeal was that she'd been the one to finally have enough fortitude to end the reckless behavior.

A brief knock on the door had her and Hank glancing around to see Brady Donovan walking into the office. A tall, lean man with tawny hair and handsome features, he'd worked as a deputy for several years and along the way been wounded in the line of duty before he'd eventually been promoted to undersheriff. Since his brother-in-law owned the

Chaparral Ranch, she knew that solving the arson case was of utmost importance to him.

"You two have anything new to report?" he asked.

"Not yet," Hank spoke up. "I still have several more people to interview on the Chaparral. The employee roster for that place is huge. You want me to include the women working in the business office, too?"

Brady said, "Everyone means everyone."

"Seems like a waste of time to me. I can't see a secretary or file clerk dragging a jug of gasoline into the forest and setting the place ablaze."

"Maybe you can't envision it, but I can," Brady told him. "Anyway, women gossip. The office workers might have over-head remarks that could be helpful."

The undersheriff leveled a pointed look at Rosalinda. "And before you say anything, men gossip, too. So have you un-covered anything interesting yet?"

"I'm about to type up my notes and go over them a second time. So far I've not found anything suspicious concerning the Pine Ridge Ranch hands. But I need to cross-reference all their statements to see if I can pick up any inconsisten-cies. And I've not interviewed the cook yet."

"He should have been the first man on your list. The one person who can tell you the most about a group of men is the one who feeds them."

"Oh, you mean the bunkhouse cook." She tapped a pen-cil on her open notebook. "I've already had a lengthy dis-cussion with him. I'm talking about Ty—er, Mr. Pickens's house cook. Gib is his name. I'll have to make another trip out there, I suppose."

"No supposing about it. You're going this morning."

Rosalinda looked at him with surprise. "This morning? You think Gib is that important?"

"I'm not sending you out there to talk to him. I want you to take a look at the spot where the fire originated."

Another trip to the Pine Ridge Ranch today. The order had Rosalinda unconsciously bracing herself. "I thought the fire marshal and his team had gone all over that area. What can I do?"

"Look over the layout of the land. Take pictures. See if you can figure out the easiest trail in and out of the area and how convenient it might have been for someone to reach it. From the Chaparral ranch yard and the Pine Ridge. Use your head. You'll know what to look for whenever you get there."

Since she'd not seen the spot where the fire had originated, she had no idea how short or far a distance it was from the road. "Will I need to hike to reach this spot or can I drive the four-wheel drive?" she asked.

"From what the fire marshal told me, it's at least a mile off the road. Drive as far as you can. Hike the rest. I'll give you the information to load into your GPS."

Rosalinda rose to her feet while across from her Hank asked Brady, "You want me to go with her? She might get lost."

"Lost? Hell," Brady said with sarcasm that was only used between good friends. "You're the one who needs navigation lessons. I'd hate to count the times you've been lost."

"Well, you've not always been perfect yourself, Brady Donovan," Hank said with a roll of his eyes.

Hank could get away with that sort of talk to the undersheriff. Before Brady had been promoted, the two men had worked as partners for years and they remained steadfast buddies. Even so, Hank understood he could only push Brady so far before he got himself into real trouble.

"Not with you riding in the same truck with me," Brady quipped, motioning for Rosalinda to follow him. Once they reached the door, he tossed back at Hank, "And don't leave the building without seeing me. I have more for you to do, too."

After Brady had given her the information she needed to locate the fire spot, she gathered her equipment and began the long drive to the Pine Ridge Ranch.

Thirty miles and many more minutes later, she was driving the dirt road that led to Tyler's property when she spotted a white truck traveling toward her. From the distance between them, it was impossible to identify the driver, but the truck looked exactly like the one she'd seen the rancher driving yesterday morning.

Her heart racing at a ridiculous speed, she lifted her foot off the gas and eased the vehicle over onto the shoulder of the road. Moments later, the truck pulled alongside her and the window rolled down to reveal the dark, rugged rancher behind the steering wheel.

Even though his eyes were covered with sunglasses, she could tell he was surprised to see her.

"What are you doing here?"

His mind was in the present, thank God. So why couldn't she yank hers off last night and the way his lips had felt? Why was she looking at him now and wondering how it would feel to be his lover?

Trying to ward off a shiver of excitement, she said, "Undersheriff Donovan has given me another assignment this morning. I've got to hike over to where the fire originated and look over the area."

"Why?"

"It might give us clues to add to more clues. Every piece of evidence helps complete the puzzle."

He pulled off his aviators and looked at her. "Well, I don't know what the hell you could find up there that the fire marshal didn't find. But you don't need to be hiking that distance.

The terrain is as rough as a corncob and the day is already getting hot."

"If it's too rough to drive, I'll have to hike," she reasoned.

"No. I'll turn around and you follow me back to the ranch. I'll take you there on horseback. Do you know how to ride?"

From the moment she'd spotted him her nerves had gone on alert. Now they were stretched so tight they were humming with high tension. "Sure. I used to ride a lot when I was younger."

He nodded. "Good. Then it's settled."

This was not the way she'd planned for things to go, Rosalinda thought. Hank was already accusing her of fraternizing with a suspect. If he found out about this, it would only add fuel to the fire. But being in Tyler's company wasn't a crime, she assured herself. Even if it might be a danger.

"Weren't you on your way out?" she asked. "I wouldn't want to interrupt your morning."

"The errand I was going to run isn't that important," he assured her. "Just wait until I turn around and I'll follow you up to the ranch yard."

He didn't give her time to protest. Instead, he drove on to leave her sitting there wondering if fate was trying to play a hand against her. The last thing she needed was to spend any more time with a man who continually reminded her she was a woman with needs. Ones that only a man could satisfy.

Forget the urges, Rosalinda. Just remember that Tyler Pickens obviously has problems of his own. Something clearly drove a wedge between him and his family. Could be that something was a woman. You don't want to become part of this man's problems. And you sure don't want to have to deal with another stalker like Monique.

Her lips pressed to a grim line, Rosalinda watched his

truck approaching her from the rear. Like it or not, she was going to have to make this trek with the man and keep herself under control while she was doing it.

Chapter Five

Ten minutes later, they arrived at the Pine Ridge Ranch yard. After plucking up a small backpack holding the few items she needed to take with her, she left the truck and found Tyler waiting for her a few steps away from the tailgate.

He said, "Let's walk down to the horse barn and I'll find something suitable for you to ride. In the meantime, did you bring any lunch with you?"

"Lunch? It's only ten o'clock. It won't take us that long to get to the site and back, will it?"

"It's not that far in distance, but the roughness makes it slow going. Probably an hour in and another to come back out," he answered.

"Well, I've got a candy bar in my backpack. That's enough to keep me going."

He shook his head. "That won't do. I'll have Gib bring us down something while I saddle the horses."

The man was clearly taking over and she needed to open

her mouth and tell him to back off. But this was his ranch, she reasoned. And if he was willing to extend her a little help, she wasn't going to protest.

As they walked the fifty yards or so to the stables, Tyler called the house cook and gave him a few short orders. By the time Tyler had a black gelding saddled for himself and a handsome paint for her, Gib showed up with a pair of saddlebags packed with food and drinks.

After the older man had handed the leather pouches over to Tyler, he turned to Rosalinda. "Good mornin', Deputy. I didn't expect to see you again so soon."

Rosalinda offered him her hand, and he gave it a warm, hearty shake. "Good morning, Gib. I'm sorry my appearance caused you extra work. I told Tyler not to bother. But he ignored me."

The cook's gaze slid thoughtfully over to his boss. "Tyler tends to do that. He has a mind of his own."

"So does someone else I know," Tyler commented, as he adjusted the latigo on Rosalinda's mount.

Rosalinda's gaze encompassed both men. "Have you two known each other for long?" she asked Gib.

The older man chuckled. "I held Tyler in my arms the day he was born. That's how long we've known each other."

"Oh. Then he must be like a son to you," Rosalinda commented while her thoughts went back to Tyler's remarks about leaving his family behind in Texas. Apparently, this man had chosen to leave Texas, too. Out of love and loyalty to Tyler? she wondered. Or because of some sort of shared problem back there?

"Yes, ma'am, he is. I've whipped his britches a time or two."

Tyler chuckled. "You mean you tried."

Grinning, Gib tossed her a wink. "Damned little rascal was always kicking me in the shins."

Rosalinda smiled at his teasing. "I hope he's grown out of that sort of mischief."

"Sometimes I wish he hadn't," Gib replied. "I liked him better when he was a naughty tyke."

Before Rosalinda could make any sort of reply, Tyler led both horses forward. As he passed the cook, he shot the man a dry look. "And I like you better when you're seen and not heard."

Unaffected by Tyler's sarcasm, Gib looked over at Rosalinda and smiled. "Stick around a while, deputy, and you'll soon learn he's a real sweetheart."

"Thanks for the advice, Gib. And if I have time when we get back from this ride, I'd like to talk to you about the fire."

"Anytime, Deputy Lightfoot. I'll be glad to help if I can."

As the older man ambled away, Rosalinda looked at the rancher. A sweetheart? At the moment the gelding he was about to ride had a nicer expression on his face than Tyler. But that didn't put her off. Last night she'd learned there was a tender side to this man and she couldn't help but wonder if or when he might show that part of himself to her again.

"Don't pay any attention to Gib," Tyler told her. "He's always full of bull."

She took the reins he offered her. "I like him. He reminds me of my Grandfather Lightfoot. He's still going strong at age ninety. If you're lucky, Gib will be, too."

"Yeah. I hope my old friend will be around for a long, long time." He gestured to an open spot a short distance away. "Let's walk them out there and get mounted. We've got a long ride ahead."

Once they were safely away from the stable area, Rosalinda looped the handle of her backpack over the saddle horn, then levered the reins over the animal's head. "What is this paint's name?" she asked him.

"Moonpie. And he doesn't have any bad habits except

grabbing a mouthful of grass or leaves whenever he gets the chance."

"Okay, Moonpie," she said to the horse. "Be a good boy and take care of me." She was about to put her foot in the stirrup when Tyler suddenly came up behind her and clamped his hands around her waist.

"Let me help you," he said lowly. "Moonpie is a tall guy."

The touch of his hands sent heat radiating through her upper body and urged her to turn and bring her face close to his, but she was determined to keep her eyes straight ahead and focused instead on lifting herself into the leather seat.

"Thanks," she murmured once she was safely settled atop the horse.

His fingers rested on her stirrup, so near to the toe of her boot that she could very nearly feel them.

"Good thing you wore boots today. But is the pistol necessary?"

"I wear boots and the pistol every day," she replied. "The weapon is a required part of the uniform. And it might come in handy."

He let out a long breath. "Yeah. Who knows, we might see a snake along the way."

Whether he was talking about the two-legged kind or one that crawled on its belly, she wasn't sure. Either way, she got the impression that her weapon unsettled him. "Does the pistol bother you for some reason?"

"Not exactly. It just looks out of place on such a—lovely woman like you."

She'd not expected anything like that to come out of his mouth any more than she'd expected his compliment to fill her with such warm pleasure.

"Flattering an officer of the law will get you nowhere," she murmured.

He pushed the brim of his hat back slightly on his forehead

as a sly grin crinkled the corners of his eyes and curved his lips. "I wasn't flattering the officer part—just the woman."

A long, shaky breath eased out of her. In her line of work she'd dealt with all sorts of men. But she'd never encountered one quite like Tyler, and to say that his presence shook her would be a ridiculous understatement.

"Well, the officer part is saying we need to get going," she said.

He tugged the brim of his hat back onto his forehead, then gave the toe of her boot a companionable pat. "Okay. Let's head 'em up and move 'em out."

Once he was comfortably astride Inky, the black gelding, they turned the horses in a southerly direction and eased them into a long trot. As she watched the distant tree line grow closer, it suddenly dawned on Rosalinda that he'd not bothered to consult her about the GPS directions. Of course he would know the general area of the burn. But how could he know the exact spot of ignition? she wondered.

"Don't you think you'd better follow my GPS?" she asked as she strove to get her body to relax and go with the rhythmic rise and fall of the horse's gait.

"No need for that."

"So you know where the fire originally ignited?"

"I haven't been there since the fire, if that's what you're asking. Sheriff Hamilton informed me this morning as to where the fire began and I'm familiar with the spot he's talking about. Before I talked with him I wasn't sure if the flames had started on my ranch or the Chaparral. And I'm grateful to him for letting me know. You didn't tell me yesterday," he added in a faintly accusing tone.

She glanced over at him and couldn't help thinking how at home he looked in the saddle and the easy way his body blended with the horse. No doubt he'd grown up in this type of life and whatever had occurred back in Texas hadn't pulled him away from it.

You're thinking too much about this man, Rosa. You need to be concentrating on the fire that blazed across hundreds of acres, instead of the fire he's building in you.

Giving herself a mental shake, she said, "I didn't have the authority to give you that information."

"So you don't break the rules," he stated. "That's good to know."

Was he talking about more than her job? What other rules could he be talking about? Rules of life? Courtship or marriage?

Even though her mind was screaming at her to forget the innuendo, she couldn't help but ask. "What about you? Do you break the rules?"

He shot her a clever grin. "Not yet. But I've been tempted."

Since his remark only confused her more, she didn't make any sort of reply and for the next few minutes they rode in silence.

The summer sun was already hot in the morning sky and by the time they rode beneath a copse of tall cottonwoods, the shade felt cool against her bare arms and face. Here the trees, grass and underbrush were lush and green, telling her they were still a long distance from where flames had wreaked havoc with the land. Birds were twittering overhead, while a breeze faintly ruffled the leaves. The sound of creaking leather mixed with the occasional clank of a metal horseshoe against stone. Somewhere in the near distance a cow bawled to her calf. The natural sounds were soothing to her, and she decided Brady had done her a favor by sending her on this little mission.

"It's beautiful here," Rosalinda spoke her thoughts aloud. "The trees are like a green roof with hundreds of tiny skylights."

He looked over at her. “Well, I’d have more grazing land if I took out the trees, but they work as shelter for the cattle. Especially during the winter months.”

“I expect the snow gets fairly deep up here,” she remarked. “What happens to the cattle then? Do you move them to a barn or something?”

Smiling patiently, he shook his head. “I’d have to build a dozen more barns to do that. No. When the weather is bad, we make sure the herds are all off the mountain ranges and locked down on the flats. They find shelter in the arroyos and brush. And we spread feed and hay to them on a daily basis.”

“I see. That must be a huge task. You probably hope it never snows.”

“On the contrary. The snow helps moisture and nutrients seep right into the roots of the grass. So it, in turn, helps feed the cattle.” He made a sweeping gesture to the area around them. “God knew what he was doing when he made all of this.”

And He’d certainly known what He was doing when He made Tyler Pickens, Rosalinda couldn’t help thinking. Everything, from his jet-black hair and sunbaked skin, to his long, sinewy body, was eye-catching, and she had no doubt that wherever he went female gazes would follow.

So why weren’t any of those females around? Rosalinda wondered. The man was young, yet past the age when most men take a wife and started a family. That could have already happened, her thoughts ventured on. Could be it was a wife and children he’d left behind in Texas? No. He might leave a woman, she decided, but she couldn’t picture this man walking away from a child.

“You must be very proud of your ranch.”

“Damn right. I’ve worked long years to make it what it is today. And those first few years were lean times. Very lean. I only had Gib, Sawyer and Tobey to help me. I couldn’t afford to hire dozer work so most of the meadows we cleared by hand. And we ate beans until I thought I'd turn into one." He shrugged as though he'd put the memories of those hard times behind him. "But it was all worth it."

"My folks always told us kids that worthwhile things rarely come easy. And I guess my job has taught me the truth of that motto. Most days are never easy, but it's all worthwhile."

A faint grin slanted his lips. "Well, I'll do my best to make part of this day easy for you. It's the least I can do to help you catch the creep who decided to play with matches."

He urged the black gelding into another long trot and Rosalinda had no choice but to follow.

During the next half hour, the landscape continually changed from thick woods to open meadows, to river bottom land, then back to steep gullies and rough washes. Because of her job, Rosalinda worked out at the gym on a regular basis and made sure she was in the best of shape, but by the time they'd traveled about forty-five minutes every muscle in her body was aching with fatigue. Brady must have been out of his mind thinking she could reach this area by foot, she thought. But then it might have been much closer if she'd started from the main road instead of the Pine Ridge Ranch yard.

Just when Rosalinda thought she couldn't go any farther, Tyler pulled his horse to a stop and motioned for her to do the same. For the past few minutes the landscape had turned even rougher with huge slabs of rock jutting from the ground at precarious slants. The underbrush was thick and scrubby while most of the ground was covered with huge patches of prickly pear. Presently, the cacti were blooming bright yellow roses, making her wish she could pull out the department camera and snap photos of the beautiful sight. But Brady would hardly appreciate her attention straying to flowers.

"There's a bluff up ahead," Tyler announced. "It would

be safer for us and the horses if we dismount and walk the rest of the way."

"Fine with me," Rosalinda agreed. "As much as I like Moonpie, I need a break from the saddle."

He swiftly swung himself to the ground and walked over to give her a helping hand off the horse's back. Once she was standing on the ground, she realized there was much more than the beautiful cactus blooms distracting her. Having Tyler standing so close, with his hand resting on her arm, was like watching an approaching tornado, while knowing there was no path of escape. The thrill of oncoming danger was almost more than she could bear.

"Are you okay?" He ducked his head just a fraction so that he could look directly into her face. "Your legs aren't going to buckle on me, are they?"

Even as he asked the question, she could feel his fingers tightening on her arm. His concern made her feel special and oh, so womanly. And suddenly she found it hard to breathe. Hard to do anything except gaze into his green eyes.

"I'm okay. Just a little wobbly," she finally managed to say, letting out a nervous little laugh. "I thought my legs were in great shape. I run several miles a week. But right now they feel like a wet sponge."

His gentle smile said he understood completely. "Riding uses muscles that running and other exercises don't. I should've stopped sooner and given you a break." He gestured to an area just ahead of them. "Let's walk over there. It will help loosen your muscles."

She nodded and he promptly closed a firm hold around her elbow. As he helped her over the rough ground, Rosalinda could have told him that his touch made her knees just as weak as their morning ride. But that would be the same as admitting that she was more than attracted to him. And she couldn't do that. She wasn't ready to allow a man to enter her life again.

"What about the horses? Shouldn't we tether them to a bush or something?" She voiced the questions as they walked away from the animals.

"They've been taught to be ground-tied. They won't go anywhere until we come back for them."

"Smart horses."

"I wouldn't have any other kind on the ranch."

What about women? she wondered, before mentally shaking herself. He'd been a bachelor for several years. That ought to be enough answer for her wandering mind.

By the time they reached the edge of the bluff, most of the strength had returned to Rosalinda's legs, but she wasn't at all sure her sanity was intact. She kept telling herself that she didn't need his support and to move away from him, but her body refused to follow the message in her head.

"Be careful here," Tyler warned. "The ground is very loose here. I don't want you falling."

Craning her neck, Rosalinda peered down to see a drop of thirty feet or more. At the bottom everything was black and burned to a crisp. "Oh, my, that's a long and dangerous drop. Is that where the fire started? Down there?"

"When Sheriff Hamilton described the place to me I didn't have to wonder. My ranch includes several thousand acres, but there's no other spot on it like this one. Before the fire it was beautiful. Now it's a wasteland."

There was a touch of anger in his voice, but mostly there was disappointment. And the sadness in his eyes was something that couldn't be faked. If she'd had any suspicions about the man being involved with the arson before, they were totally gone with the wind now.

"So this area we see below us is still on your ranch?" she asked.

"That's right. But the Chaparral fence is only a short distance away," he told her. "We'll go down so that you can see the layout for yourself."

"But how do we get down there? You might be able to scale this steep wall, but I'm not sure I can."

"I wouldn't let you try such a thing. There's a trail to our left. It's rough. But the cattle and wildlife manage to use it."

With his hand still on her arm, he started to lead her away, but Rosalinda felt compelled to turn to him.

"Just a minute, Tyler. There's something I think I should tell you."

Pausing, he smiled down at her. "You called me Tyler," he said.

His voice was like water moving over a gravel bed. Smooth, yet rough at the same time. The sound of it sent a rush of pleasure through her and before she could stop it a blush flooded her face with color. "I guess I did, didn't I?"

"I liked it, too."

She gave her lips a nervous lick. "Well, I just wanted to say that I don't believe you had anything to do with this crime."

He let out a humorous grunt. "Trying to draw flies with honey?" he asked.

Tossing him a sardonic glance, she said, "I didn't have to tell you my feelings. In fact, a smart and crafty deputy would have kept her mouth shut. So I suppose I've broken one of those rules you were talking about earlier."

He turned just enough to face her head-on and as he met her gaze, his hand released her elbow and slid slowly, provocatively up to her shoulder.

"So why did you?" he asked, his voice a low rumble.

An array of emotions rushed at her from all directions, forcing her to swallow before she could speak. "I can't tell you exactly why. I suppose because I like you. To be honest, I'm beginning to think I like you a little too much."

His cool green eyes suddenly took on a warm glow. "And I like you, Rosa."

She breathed deeply. "I'm not sure what any of that means. Or where it leaves us."

The twist of his lips had her gaze zeroing in on his mouth and the remembered taste of him caused her heart to pound with anticipation.

"It leaves us right here," he said huskily. "Together. Like this."

There was no sense in trying to dodge his descending head. Ever since last night, she'd thought of little else but his kiss. And every time she'd thought of it, she'd realized she'd wanted to relive those moments of pleasure again.

"We didn't ride all the way out here for this," she whispered the feeble protest.

"Maybe not," he murmured. "But we don't want the trip to be wasted, now do we?"

His lips blotted out any sort of answer she could have given him. But she swiftly decided that words between them no longer mattered. His plundering kiss was coaxing her lips open and urging her arms to slide around his waist.

Somewhere in her foggy daze, she heard his groan and the sound was so intoxicating she wasn't even aware that her body was arching into his or that her hands were gripping the sides of his waist. Her heated response sent his tongue thrusting between her teeth and searching the moist concave of her mouth.

The intimate taste of him totally consumed her. So much so that if they'd toppled over the edge of the cliff she would have gladly fallen with him. And that could only mean she was in deep, deep trouble.

Yet even that scary realization wasn't enough to make her pull away him. For more than four years, she'd shut herself away from men and sex, from being loved and touched and pleasured. Tyler was making her see that she couldn't shut herself away any longer. No matter how much of a price she had to pay.

Chapter Six

If one of the horses hadn't whinnied, Tyler figured the kiss would have gone on forever, or until one of them had passed out from lack of oxygen. But the sound was enough to penetrate his foggy senses.

While he glanced over his shoulder at the horses, Rosalinda spoke in a breathless rush. "What's wrong? Is the horse running away?"

"Nothing is wrong. Inky realizes some of his old friends are grazing not far away. He's just doing a little talking," he explained in a husky voice.

Her shoulders visibly slumped with relief. "Oh. I was thinking someone might have walked up on us."

"And see that you weren't exactly behaving as if you were on duty?" he asked wryly.

"I don't need reminding," she muttered, then passed trembling fingers over her forehead. "I think we need to get moving on to the bottom of the bluff."

He wrapped his hand around her upper arm and though he desperately wanted to pull her back into his arms, he stopped himself short. If he kissed her again like he had a few seconds ago, he'd be a goner. There'd be no stopping until the two of them were making love.

"Rosa, a while ago you told me something you thought I ought to know. Well, it's my turn now. I—" He stopped, shook his head, then started again. "I didn't kiss you just because we're alone and the opportunity presented itself."

Dropping her head, she stared at the ground. "It doesn't matter," she said quietly.

Tyler gazed at the crown of her dark, shiny hair as he tried to gather his senses and find the right words to explain himself. But how could he expect to explain anything when he didn't know what was happening to him or why he wanted to reach for this woman every time she got within ten feet of him.

"It matters to me, Rosa. I guess because you're the first woman since—well, you're the first woman in a long, long time that has made me feel anything. I can't explain why. And I'm not even sure that the why of it has any importance. All that matters is that we've met and that something is happening between us."

Her head lifted and the dark clouds of confusion in her eyes hit him like the strike of a hammer in the middle of his chest.

"Whatever this is, Tyler, it's got to stop. It's wrong."

Wrong. When Tyler had first started dating DeeDee, his father had continually repeated that word to him. And in the end Warren Pickens had been right about the woman. She'd been all wrong for Tyler and he'd made a huge mistake in thinking she would be a good wife to him.

But did that mean he was making a mistake now with Rosalinda? No. This woman wasn't DeeDee. And Tyler hadn't needed his father's advice or support in nearly ten years. Nothing about this was the same, he mentally argued.

His hands closed over her shoulders and the heat of her flesh flowed into him like a warm drink on a cold dark night.

"Why does it need to stop, Rosa? It's just started."

Her lips began to quiver and he touched his forefinger to the moist curves. He didn't want to cause this woman any kind of anguish. He wanted to make her happy.

"This—you and me—it's compromising my job, Tyler."

"You can't be a woman and a deputy, too?"

"Not while I'm on duty," she answered glumly.

His slow smile was full of promise. "Okay. I can wait until you're off duty to kiss you."

"We won't be seeing each other when I'm off duty," she countered.

"I wouldn't count on that, Rosa." Reluctantly, he released his hold on her shoulders and gestured toward a narrow path leading between two slabs of rock. "There's the trail. If you're ready, we'll head on down."

"Let me get my camera. What about the saddlebags with our lunch?"

He shook his head. "I don't think you'd want to eat down there. We'll find a better spot for that."

She walked back over to Moonpie and fished the camera from her backpack. Once she returned and they started toward the rocks, he ordered, "Stay right behind me. That way if you fall I can stop you from tumbling to the bottom."

"Don't worry. I'll watch my step."

After several minutes of slipping and sliding down the steep trail, the two of them reached the bottom without incident. Rosalinda wiped at the sweat on her brow and looked around the blackened landscape.

The face of the bluff was at least sixty or seventy feet wide and created a natural curvature in the landscape. Tyler noticed how the flames had eaten halfway up the wall until the lack of brush and scrub trees had left it without fuel.

Rosalinda's gaze followed the direction his had taken before making a sweeping arc of the area behind them. "Everything smells like smoke and soot. And it looks—well, it's terribly sad, Tyler. It's like stepping from a beautiful garden into a barren desert. No. It's worse than that," she quickly corrected herself. "At least a desert has living creatures and plants in it. I doubt you could find anything that's alive in this."

"Well, right now the trees appear to be dead," he told her. "But I'm hoping the hardwoods will eventually leaf back out. The evergreens might not have fared so well, though." He walked closer to the rocky cliff and Rosalinda followed. "Sheriff Hamilton says the fire was set here at the very base of the cliff. And now that I'm looking at it, I'm just thankful to God that it didn't climb the face and burn toward my ranch."

"Hmm. From what I understand, on the night of the fire, the wind was out of the south and then switched to a northwesterly direction. If that hadn't happened, more of your land would have been burned instead of the Chaparral," Rosalinda mused aloud. "I wonder if the arsonist had been anticipating a wind change or if he or she had even taken the wind into account."

"That would depend on how smart he or she is," Tyler replied. "And whether the person was trying to burn me out or the Cantrells."

"That's true," Rosalinda agreed. She drew a camera from her backpack and began to snap shots from all sorts of angles.

Tyler asked, "Didn't the fire marshal take photos?"

"I'm sure he did and I think he's shared them with Sheriff Hamilton. But Brady wanted me to take some of my own.

Just to see the place from a different perspective. Can you show me where the Cantrell property starts?"

He gestured to the area directly behind them and they began to walk side by side over the scorched ground. "Sawyer has already discovered that a slew of cedar fence posts have burned and the fence is down in places. It will all have to be repaired before my cattle and Quint's cattle can run in this area again. But there's hardly a hurry to get it back up just yet. There's not a blade of grass around here for them to eat anyway. Damn it, but I'd like to get my hands on the creep who did this."

"Don't worry. He'll get his due punishment in a court of law," she said.

"If you catch him," Tyler pointed out.

"Don't say *if,* Tyler. Say *when.* Because I can assure you that Sheriff Hamilton won't shut the doors on this case until it's finished."

"You sound very resolute."

"When it comes to my job, I am," she said firmly.

Apparently, her job was everything to her, he thought. At least, it seemed to him that being a deputy took up most of her life. She certainly wasn't devoting any of it to a husband or children like most women her age. But that was her prerogative, Tyler thought. Just like his was to be a rancher. Still, there were so many things he'd like to know about the woman. But that would have to wait for a better time. When she was off duty and that shiny badge wasn't pinned to her breast.

The two of them walked less than twenty yards when they came upon the downed fence. Studying it more closely, they could see that none of the barbed wire had been cut. It had simply collapsed because there were no posts left to support the strings of wire.

"So this is the fence that separates the Pine Ridge Ranch from the Chaparral?" she asked.

Tyler used the toe of his boot to kick the wire from their path. "One of many. Our ranches butt up to each other for several miles."

"Several miles," she thoughtfully repeated. "I can't imagine anyone owning that much land. My family's farm consists of a hundred acres and that's considered large in my social circles."

He grimaced. "You make it sound like I should feel like a heel for being well-off. I thought women admired men with ambition."

"This woman admires a man with heart. The rest is unimportant."

Heart? That was the one thing his twin brother had accused him of not having. And the very description DeeDee had pinned on him. But they'd been wrong, he thought. He'd always felt deeply about people and things; he'd just kept most of it hidden. Mainly because Trent had shown enough for both of them. Now, years later, he wasn't comfortable wearing his emotions on his sleeve. Unless it was anger. Thanks to his father, that was the one thing he was good at expressing. But maybe it was time to change that, he thought. Maybe it was time he learned to let this woman, and others close to him, see that his heart was full of emotions. That he was equally capable of loving and longing and needing.

He replied, "I've been told mine is as hard as a rock."

Momentarily lowering her camera, she cast a glance at him. "I truly doubt that."

Her observation caught him totally off guard. The only person who'd ever really understood him was Gib. Could it be that Rosalinda recognized something in him that his own family hadn't acknowledged?

Hell, Tyler, you're trying to imagine things about this woman that most likely aren't there. She looks damned good to you, but that doesn't mean she'd ever love or understand you.

As he tried to push away the bitter voice in his head, he watched her snap more pictures of the adjoining Chaparral land. When she eventually turned and stared at the cliff, she said, "It looks to me like it would be a heck of a lot easier for someone to approach this area from the south. If the arsonist came from the direction of your ranch, he would have had to climb down like we just did. That would be difficult to do carrying a can or jug of accelerant."

"That's true. But the arsonist could have traveled the long way around to get here to the bluff," Tyler pointed out.

She glanced at him. "The long way?"

He nodded. "Yeah. Walk to the east or west of the cliff until he found an easier descent."

"I don't believe that happened." She turned off the camera and slipped it into her backpack. "I believe someone came up from the south, from the Chaparral, and he chose this spot because it's sheltered. Because he thought that Mother Nature and the curvature of the cliff would naturally send the fire away from you and on to Chaparral land. But the wind changed and it ended up burning a part of your land, too. He'd not counted on the wind."

"That's logical. But why bother to come all the way up here?" Tyler asked. "If this person was out to burn the Cantrell's land, why not just start it somewhere on that ranch?"

"To throw suspicion on you and your men."

Frowning, he walked over to where she stood. "Do you really think that? Or are you saying it just to loosen my guard in hopes that I'll let something incriminating slip?"

The chuckle that passed her lips was full of disbelief. "If I thought you had something incriminating to tell me I wouldn't even be here with you right now." She gestured up to the top of the cliff. "If you're ready to start back, I'm finished down here."

"Yes. Let's get back up to the horses and find a place to eat our lunch."

The climb back up the trail was even harder than going down. Rosalinda snatched and grabbed for holds on rocks and twigs, but she continued to doggedly make her way to the top.

Halfway up, she spoke between pants for air. "I can't imagine a cow coming up this trail. It would have to be part mountain goat."

"You'd be surprised at the places they can travel. The cattle and horses are the ones who made this trail. One day before the snow comes again, I'll show you some of the cattle trails that lead up into the mountain ranges. There's an old cabin up there that used to be a prospector's shack."

When they finally reached the plateau, the horses were still standing where they'd left them. Their heads were slightly bowed, their eyes half-closed as they dozed and waited for their riders to return.

To let them know he appreciated their obedience, Tyler patted each horse's neck before he retrieved the saddlebags filled with their lunch. Once he returned to Rosalinda she was wiping a hand across her sweaty brow.

"Let's find a place in the shade to sit and eat," he suggested.

"I am ready for a break," she agreed. "I think I could drink a gallon of water right now."

A few feet away from the horses, they found a rock large enough for the two of them to share. After they were seated, Tyler pulled the food and drink from the leather pouches, then handed one of the water bottles to Rosalinda.

She quickly twisted off the lid and downed half the contents. "Thanks. I feel better already."

Gib had packed roast beef sandwiches, along with corn

chips and homemade cookies that tasted like molasses. Rosalinda ate with a hearty appetite, and the sight pleased him just as much as the image of her capably riding Moonpie had. He liked that she wasn't a fragile woman, liked that she could be beautiful and strong at the same time.

"Now do you see why I was concerned about you walking all the way out here to this place?" He handed her one of the sandwiches. "It would have been a very long trek on foot."

She began to peel the cellophane off the sandwich. "But it would have been shorter to have walked from the road, wouldn't it? That's the starting point Brady used to calculate the distance. He's not going to believe that you and I rode back here together."

Surprise had him staring at her. "You're going to tell him?"

"Of course. He's one of my bosses. He has a right to know how I carried out my assignment."

Even though his stomach was gnawing with hunger, he was starving even more for the sight of her. During the climb some of her hair had caught in the brush and loosened from her ponytail. Now the escaped strands curled around her face and rested against her neck. Her rosy, tanned skin was damp with sweat, and drips of water clung to her lower lip. The urge to have those lips pressed against his gripped him like a vise.

You've been without a woman's company for too long, Tyler. You get close to this one and you start feeling like a stallion wanting to break out of his stall.

He cleared his throat. "Does he have the right to know about the kiss?

She rolled her eyes. "Just because I acted like a fool with you doesn't mean I'm completely crazy."

"Would you get fired?"

A frown pulled her brows into a straight line. "I'm not sure. Besides, he's not going to hear it from me."

She promptly bit into her sandwich and Tyler decided it

was time to focus on his lunch and forget about getting his lips or hands or anything else on this woman.

"What made you choose this place to build a ranch?" She reached for the bag of chips lying between them and poured a small amount into her palm. "Most of it appears to be mountain range. I'm not a cattleman, but seems to me like that wouldn't offer nearly as much grazing."

"You're only seeing the area where the ranch house and work yard is located. There's plenty of lower meadowland to go with it."

"So it wasn't just a piece of land you settled for. It was something you fell in love with?"

Funny that no one had ever asked him that before. Not even Gib. Not even himself. But now that she had, it made him realize exactly what his ranch had come to mean to him.

"When I first saw this land, the only thing I remember thinking was that it had potential. But now—looking back—I think I've always been in love with it. And that—well, surprises me. You see, when I left Texas I didn't expect to like any place as much or more than the one I left behind. But this land and I have grown together. It's a bond that will never break. I'll be here until I die."

"So that place in Texas—you don't ever plan to go back?"

He looked across the small plateau toward the horses. Bees buzzed around the prickly pear blooms while on a nearby spruce, a pair of bright-colored birds flitted from limb to limb. But at the moment he was only seeing part of the beauty before him. Instead, he was seeing the rolling plains of the Rocking P, the herd of cattle that he and his twin brother had shared. At one time the two of them had planned so much for the family ranch. With their father getting older, the brothers understood that someday they would own the ranch together and they would continue to build it for all the Pickens children to come. But the children hadn't come. Not for Tyler. And he would never own a part of the Rocking P again.

"No. If I did it would only be for a short visit. And I don't plan to even do that."

She ate the last chip she'd been holding, and brushed the crumbs from her hands. "So there's not anyone back there that you miss?"

The image of his mother's face swam before his eyes. She'd been a beautiful woman, but the years had marched on since he'd last seen her. He supposed her black hair was becoming threaded with gray now and her green eyes would be faintly lined with wrinkles. When things had begun to fall apart in the Pickens family, she'd been the only person, other than Gib, who'd believed in him and tried to show him support.

And Edie Pickens had suffered some hell from Warren for giving her son that much. He'd wanted his wife and the whole family to stand against Tyler. Just because he'd refused to let the old man dominate and rule his life.

Suddenly, the sound of Rosalinda's voice interrupted his thoughts. "Tyler. Is something wrong? If you'd rather not answer, that's okay with me."

"I'm fine. I was just thinking about my mother." He smiled to hide the crack in the middle of his heart. "Even though we boys grow into men, we still think of our moms. I do miss her. A lot."

"Were you close to her?"

He nodded. "I was always closer to her than my dad. Sometimes I think that's why he was always so hard on me. I didn't share things with him like I did with her. But that's a long, complicated story, Rosa. One you probably wouldn't want to hear. Even if I could tell it."

She reached over and laid her hand on his forearm and in that moment Tyler desperately wanted to draw her into his arms and simply hold her close to let her compassion and warmth restore that break in his heart.

"I'd like to hear it sometime," she said gently. "Whenever you feel like you could tell it."

He nodded, then promptly stood before the need to touch her became too strong to overpower. "If you're finished eating, we'd better be getting back. I've got an appointment with a horse buyer in Ruidoso this afternoon."

She rose to her feet and began to gather the leftovers of their simple meal. "Yes. I need to get back, too," she agreed.

Once they reached the horses and he'd fastened the saddlebags behind the cantle of his saddle, he walked around to help Rosalinda mount up.

"There's no need for you to give me a hand. I can manage."

In spite of her insistence, he locked his hands on the sides of her waist. "I'm sure you can. But it's easier with a little help, isn't it?"

"Yes. It's easier." She glanced at him only for a second before turning her gaze back to the horse's side. Tyler expected her to immediately place her foot in the stirrup, but instead, she turned to face him and from her torn expression he could plainly see she wanted to get something off her mind.

"What is it? What's wrong?" he asked.

She shook her head. "Nothing. I— Well, when I said I acted like a fool for kissing you. That wasn't exactly what I meant. I mean, that was a cruel thing for me to say. Especially when I was enjoying it as much or more than you were."

It was damned crazy, Tyler thought, but suddenly the sun seemed brighter, the sky much bluer.

"More?" he asked with an impish grin. "Somehow I doubt that, Rosa."

She glanced away from him and swallowed and as he watched the movement of her throat, he could easily imagine himself trailing a path of kisses down her neck and between her breasts. Slipping off her clothes and laying her back on his bed.

"Well. I'm not a mean person, Tyler. And I'm not a tease."

"I didn't think you were either. I think you're more worried than anything."

He could see by the faint widening of her eyes that he'd hit close to the mark.

"Worried about what?" she murmured the question.

"The way you're beginning to feel about me. The way I'm beginning to feel about you. You're realizing it's something neither of us can ignore."

"That's crazy," she argued. "We've only known each other for two days."

"And one night," he couldn't help adding. "Sometimes a look is all it takes. And we've done more than look."

She whirled back to the horse and jammed her boot in the stirrup. "I don't want to talk about this now."

"You're right. We'll talk about it when you're off duty. I want to have your full attention."

Chapter Seven

Even though they traveled the same trail on the ride back to the ranch yard, the trip seemed to pass more quickly to Rosalinda. Maybe that was because she had so much to occupy her mind. The more time she spent with Tyler, the stronger the pull she felt toward the man. He'd said they couldn't ignore what was happening between them. But she needed to do more than ignore it. She needed to stop it.

It was becoming clear to her that the man had secrets. He was still carrying the past around on his shoulders and she wasn't about to fall in love with a man who couldn't start fresh with her.

At the stables, Tyler turned Inky and Moonpie over to one of the wranglers to see to the horses' care. Rosalinda made use of the restroom located inside the horse barn, and then informed Tyler she needed to be leaving.

As the two walked to their trucks, which were parked next to each other at the side of the barn, she said, "I'll have to come back another day to interview Gib. The trip to the burn site took up so much time I need to get back to headquarters and let him and Sheriff Hamilton look over these photos."

"Unless he's gone to town for something, Gib is always here on the ranch," he told her. "Why don't you come tomorrow evening for supper? You can talk to him all you want."

That wouldn't exactly be doing an official interview, she thought. But the results would be the same.

She paused at the door to her truck and he stood a step away as he waited for her to reply.

"I'm not sure about my work schedule," she told him.

"We can make it lunch if need be. Or supper. Or breakfast. Just call the ranch house number and let Gib know. Okay?"

Another reason to see this man again, she thought. It wasn't what she needed. Or then again, maybe it was. Maybe once she did finally learn everything about Tyler Pickens she'd be able to forget he ever kissed her.

"Yes. I will. And thanks for taking me to the cliff. You saved me a lot of hiking."

His grin was faint but oh, so charming.

"It was my pleasure, Rosa."

Deciding she'd already said more than enough, she climbed into her truck and, after giving him a quick farewell wave, drove away from the ranch yard.

Close to an hour later, Rosalinda hurried into her office back at headquarters. To her surprise, Hank was still there and he stared at her as though she'd just returned from a trip to the moon.

"Rosa, my God, what happened to you?"

Never one to fuss with her appearance, she'd not taken the time to redo her ponytail or swipe on more lipstick. It had been more important to her to get back here with the photos she'd taken at the burn site. No doubt she looked a mess to

Hank. Her hair was worse than disheveled. Riding through the brush had pulled and torn it in every direction. And the makeup she'd began the day with had either vanished or was smeared from wiping sweat from her face.

Tucking a strand of loose hair behind her ear, she said, "Horseback riding. With Tyler Pickens."

She sat down at her desk and fished the camera from her backpack. As she connected the device to her computer, Hank crossed the small space to stand next to her chair.

"Tyler Pickens," he repeated thoughtfully. "What were you doing with him?"

"He took me to the ignition site of the fire. I'd planned on walking. But I happened to meet Tyler on the road up to the ranch and he offered to take me there on horseback."

Hank was quiet for a long stretch before he asked, "How did he know where the fire was set?"

Rosalinda looked up at her partner. Clearly, Hank was still suspicious of the rancher and that was completely understandable. They were only just beginning to piece together the information they'd so far gathered about the fire. But she sensed that Hank's disapproval was more of a jealous thing than a suspicion. As for her, she had to be honest with herself. It was impossible for her to think of Tyler as an arsonist or even a suspect. She could only think of him as a man who made her pulse race and her heart want to dream again.

"Sheriff Hamilton told him."

Hank groaned with disbelief. "You kiddin'? Why give information about a crime to a suspect? Ethan's been sheriff for so long he's started to crack under the strain. That or raising two sets of twins is getting him down. He says twin girls are more stressful than boys!"

All sorts of sarcastic remarks flooded onto Rosalinda's tongue, but she somehow managed to bite them back. "Sheriff Hamilton's mind is sharper than all the rest of us greenhorns in this department rolled together," she said with crisp certainty. "The fire was initially set on Tyler's land. Albeit just by a few yards. So I'm assuming Sheriff Hamilton felt Tyler had a right to know that the crime had been committed on the Pine Ridge Ranch. Besides, it's not like it's a secret. The fire marshal and his crew were all over that place."

The photos of the cliff and surrounding area were rapidly appearing on the computer screen and Rosalinda leaned forward to get a better view.

From the corner of her eye, she saw Hank crossing his arms across his chest and tapping his toe in a suggestive way. "Ah. So you're already calling him by his first name. Sounds like you're getting to know the man."

Rosalinda purposely kept her focus on the computer screen. "So what's wrong with that?"

"I'm not exactly sure. But there must be something wrong with it."

After leaving Gallop and the shelter of her family, after fighting her way out of the dangerous web that Dale and his ex-lover had caught her up in, Rosalinda had been drained both mentally and physically. But once she'd settled on the reservation, the fact that she was on her own had proved to be a tonic. Slowly but surely, she'd emerged a much more independent woman who could stand on her own. One who wasn't going to let anyone or anything control her again. And that included a possessive partner.

Her jaw tight, she said, "I thought I made it clear to you yesterday that my personal business is none of yours."

"I remember. But the fact that you're a rookie and need some guidance hasn't changed. You need—"

"My being a rookie doesn't give you the right to order me around and—"

"What in hell is going on in here?"

At the sound of Brady's voice, Rosalinda's head jerked

around to see the undersheriff entering the small workplace and from the frown on his face, he'd overheard their bickering voices.

"Nothin'," Hank quickly answered. "We were just having a discussion. About the fire."

Rosalinda turned a desperate look on Brady. "May I speak with you alone? It's something personal."

Brady's gaze encompassed both of the deputies before he sent a silent message to Hank to leave the room. After the other man had reluctantly moved into the hallway, Brady shut the door and turned to Rosalinda.

"Okay. Hank's out of earshot. So what's the problem? Him?"

Feeling like a rat fink or worse, Rosalinda shook her head. "Not exactly. Hank is—"

"You don't have to explain Hank to me," he interrupted. "I worked side by side with him for several years. He means well, but he can get under your skin at times. He never stays on course and he has a terrible habit of putting his nose where it doesn't belong. All I can say is that you have to learn his ways and try to overlook them."

"It's not any of that, Brady. It's, well—Hank did bring this up and now that he has I thought I'd better talk it over with you. To make sure I've not stepped out of bounds." As she spoke the last words a wave of heat rushed up her throat and over her face. No doubt her cheeks were red and her boss was taking note of the fact.

"So what have you done that's got Hank hopping around like a bantam rooster?"

At any other time Rosalinda would have smiled at Brady's description of her partner. Now nerves were making it impossible to relax any part of her body.

"I ate dinner last night with Tyler Pickens."

The undersheriff shrugged one shoulder. "The man has a right to eat wherever he wants to. So do you."

A long shuddering breath rushed out of her. "Today I didn't walk to the fire site. I happened to meet Tyler on the road and he took me there on horseback. Was that wrong?"

This information put a thoughtful arch to Brady's brows. "Did he tamper with evidence or try to influence any of the information you relay to the department? Or try to sway your opinion about the crime to his way of thinking?"

Shaking her head, she said, "Not at all. We mostly talked about other things. Personal things."

"Oh. I see."

"Well, is it wrong for me to get to know Tyler? As a person?"

"So this is something you want to do?"

Feeling like a blushing schoolgirl, she nodded. "I'd be lying if I said I wasn't attracted to the man. But believe me, Brady. I wouldn't let that interfere with my work. If it turned out he was guilty of anything, I could cuff him and haul him in just like anyone else. I wouldn't take pleasure in it, but I could do it."

Brady sat down in Hank's desk chair and swiveled it so that he was facing Rosalinda. "I don't believe that's anything you'll ever have to do."

She felt like a rock had suddenly landed in the pit of her stomach. "Why? You're going to take me off the case?"

Smiling faintly, the undersheriff shook his head. "No. Not hardly. You're doing a good job, Rosalinda. Just stay on track and everything will be fine. As for Tyler, Ethan and I have already crossed him off the suspect list, along with Quint and Laramie, of course. The three men are obviously victims in all this."

The relief that flooded through her was so great, her shoulders slumped back against her chair. "So it's not a problem if I get to know Tyler better?"

Brady gave her a meaningful grin. "Hank is obviously the one who's having a problem with it. But he'll get over it."

"I like Hank. I really do. But he knows the department rules. And even if we were allowed to fraternize, well—he's a good guy. But I'm not attracted to him in that way."

"Don't worry about it. Hank just needs someone in his life. He knows it can't be you. But that doesn't stop him from acting like a big brother. Once he gets attached to someone, he hangs on like gum to a shoe."

She nodded. "I've sort of figured that out. So please don't reprimand him, Brady. I don't want that."

"Don't fret about it, Rosalinda. It's all forgotten." His expression turned serious as he carefully studied her face. "So this thing with you and Tyler Pickens, you think it might turn into something special?"

Brady Donovan was a happily married man with two young children who at the same time managed to cope with a very stressful job. Rosalinda admired him greatly as a lawman and a family man. She appreciated his opinion and advice on everything.

"Well—yes—maybe." Sighing, she reached up and swiped the messy strands of hair away from her face. "I've told you all about Dale and Monique, so you can imagine I'm a bit gun-shy about starting up anything serious with him or any man just yet."

"I understand where you're coming from, but I seriously doubt that Tyler Pickens has a scorned woman around here just waiting to get revenge by stalking you."

"Spoken out loud it sounds insane, doesn't it?" Sighing, she shook her head. "I guess that's why I couldn't believe I was in any danger when it first started happening. It's still hard for me to believe anyone—especially a woman—could be so fanatical and vindictive."

"People get messed up for one reason or another. In this job you see them every day. You've learned that now, Rosa. And trust me, you won't make the same mistake twice."

"I hope you're right," she told him. "But there's a heck of a lot about Tyler Pickens that I don't know."

"Well, it could be that solving this case might give you the answers you need to know about the man," he said. Swiftly changing gears, he gestured toward the computer screen. "Are those the photos you took at the burn location?"

Glad to get back to business, she nodded. "I have some interesting things to show you."

"Good. I'm anxious to see them. And Rosalinda, it might help you to know that when I fell in love with my wife, I'd found her on the side of the road having lost her memory. I didn't know if Lass had come from Mars or a nearby jail. Or even if she was married. I went with my gut instinct and never regretted it." With that sage advice, he went over to the door and yelled down the hallway, "Get in here, Hank. It's time you do a little work around here."

The next evening a shooting at a local bar prompted Rosalinda and Hank to work overtime. As soon as she'd found a spot to pause for a couple of minutes, she'd called Gib and informed him that she wouldn't be able to make dinner. The next evening her self-defense class was scheduled for seven o'clock, so she'd not been able to make the trip to the Pine Ridge Ranch that night, either. But this evening Rosalinda was free and she'd called Gib earlier in the day to let the cook know she'd be coming.

Now as she drove the thirty miles to the ranch she had butterflies in her stomach and every five minutes she caught herself glancing down at her dress. Was Tyler going to realize she'd purposely worn it for him? And would Gib take her questions seriously once he saw her out of uniform?

By the time she parked near the sprawling ranch house, all doubts and questions suddenly fled her mind. The only thing that really mattered was that she was going to see Tyler again and she was going to let herself enjoy the evening.

Gib answered her knock and quickly ushered her into a foyer paneled with cedar and furnished with a wooden park bench, along with several potted succulents.

"It's good that you could finally make it, Miss Lightfoot. It's not often that I have a guest to cook for."

"I hope I'm not causing you extra work," she told the older man.

"Not at all." He gestured for her to precede him into a large living area. "Tyler is still out with the men. But I expect he'll be gettin' back soon. He mentioned that you wanted to ask me some questions about the fire. Come on back to the kitchen. We can talk while I finish my cooking."

"Sure. I'd like that."

The long living room was beautifully furnished with leather furniture done in oxblood-red and creamy tans. Oil paintings of Western landscapes and wildlife adorned the walls, while bright Navajo rugs were scattered across the oak floor. At the far end was a huge stone fireplace with a wide hearth flanked by two matching rockers. Since it was the middle of summer, there was obviously no need for a fire. But in the winter she could picture Tyler sitting there alone, staring into the flames.

When she and Gib entered the L-shaped kitchen, the space smelled of spices and simmering beef. Rosalinda couldn't resist sniffing the air. "Mmm. That smell is mouthwatering," she told Gib.

A modest grin came over his wrinkled features. "Better wait and taste it before you say anything else," he jokingly warned. "I'm not a real cook. I just became one out of necessity." He gestured to a table situated a few steps away from a sliding glass door. "Might as well sit and make yourself comfortable. How about a glass of iced tea or a cup of coffee?"

She sat down in a chair that allowed her a view of the lawn and the ranch yard in the distance. At the moment the only movement she spotted there was one lone cowboy carrying a feed bucket. "Tea would be nice. But only a small one. I want to save room for food."

She watched Gib fetch the drink and noticed there was a faint limp to his carriage. Unless he'd just started limping that week, one thing was certain: this man couldn't have climbed down the cliff trail to set a fire.

After he placed the glass in front of her, he returned to a large gas range where several iron pots sat on burners. He removed a lid on the largest one and poked at the contents with a long-handled fork. "So what was it you wanted to ask me about the fire, Deputy Lightfoot? I'm not sure I can be of any help. But I'll try."

"Please, call me Rosa," she instructed. "And I don't expect you have any direct information to give me. Otherwise you would have already told me about it. But maybe you could tell me how you feel about the men who work here on the ranch. You think any of them might be harboring a grudge against the Cantrells?"

With a puzzled frown, he put the lid back on the pot and lowered the flame beneath it. "The Cantrells? I figured you were thinking someone might have done this out of spite against Tyler. To make it look like he was trying to burn out the Cantrells."

That was one of the motives that she, Brady and Hank had discussed as they'd studied the photos she'd taken of the burn site. "It very well could have happened that way. Does

Tyler have any enemies around here that would go to such lengths to hurt him?"

Gib thoughtfully stroked his chin. "Tyler's ranch hands have all been working for him for several years now. Ain't none of them ever been that kind of mad at Tyler. Or anybody else for that matter. 'Course, I can't say the same for the folks back in Texas."

Gib's last comment perked her ears and not just from the standpoint of a deputy. "Oh. He had enemies back there?"

He walked over to where she sat at the table and glanced behind her as though to make sure Tyler hadn't slipped into the room. "I'd sure as hell call 'em enemies. Ain't no way I would've called 'em family."

Trying not to appear too eager, she casually sipped her tea before she presented her next question. "Tyler has hinted that he had a rift with his family."

The old man grimaced. "More than a rift, Rosa. It was a blowup. But I'd best not go into all of that with you. Ty wouldn't appreciate me talkin' about his private life. Besides, none of that has anything to do with the troubles here. I just wish that—well, that Tyler could forget it all. He tries to let on like it don't matter anymore. But that's just an act."

Thoughtful now, she wiped a finger down her sweaty glass. "Tell me, Gib, how did you happen to come out here to New Mexico with Tyler?"

He walked back over to the gas range and after checking the contents in a smaller pot, turned off the fire beneath it.

"That's easy enough to answer," he said. "Sink or swim, I wanted to be with Tyler. He's always been like my son. And I felt like he needed me."

The man's statement didn't surprise her. It was easy to see that Gib was devoted to Tyler. "Do you have any children of your own?"

"A daughter, Venus. She lives back east in Virginia. Her husband is a navy man. I rarely ever see her, though."

"And your wife?"

"She died a long time ago. When Venus was eighteen. Back then, I was still working on the Rocking P—that's the Pickens ranch in Texas. After her mother died, Venus left to go to college and then she got married. She never did like ranching life. I guess it always stood between me and her."

He gave Rosalinda a wan smile and it dawned on her that this man had suffered his own disappointments, yet he was still capable of smiling and looking forward. That took courage. She knew that well.

"I'm sorry about that, Gib."

He waved a dismissive hand at her. "Don't be. She's happy. And that's all I want. Besides, I have Ty. He ain't my blood kin, but I love him a hell of a lot more than his own daddy ever did."

Rosalinda could have pushed Gib to say more about the family issue, but she wouldn't. Like Gib had said, that information had nothing to do with the fire. And she'd rather hear the story from Tyler and know that he found her worthy of sharing it with.

"This has nothing to do with the fire either, Gib. But I noticed you have a slight limp. Did you hurt yourself?"

He returned to the table and eased down in the chair opposite her. Outside the glass doors, the sun had disappeared and shadows were spreading long fingers across the yard and beyond. Darkness would surely be driving Tyler back to house soon, she thought.

"Yeah, it happened about twelve years ago," he said. "Can't remember exactly. Time gets away from a person. Anyway, I was a regular hand then. We were branding cattle one day and I was in the midst of dragging a calf to the fire when my horse broke in two and—"

"Broke in two!" Rosalinda interrupted with a gasp. "I hope that doesn't mean what it sounds like."

Gib chuckled. "Sorry. That's cowboy lingo. It means the horse started bucking. Anyway, I ended up in a rock pile with my pelvis busted up pretty good. The accident left me with a little limp, but I could still rope and ride with the best of 'em. Warren didn't see it that way, though. He put me to work mucking horse stalls like I was nothin'. Like I hadn't given forty years of my life to that damned place."

Rosalinda could feel Gib's sense of betrayal and hurt, and her heart went out to the man. "If you could still do your work, then what was his reasoning for the demotion?"

Gib snorted. "I'd become a liability, Rosa. Too old—that's why I'd gotten bucked off, he said. The damned bastard knew that was a lie. He was a tightwad, that's the reason I was riding a bronc in the first place. He kept cheap, untrained horses around to save buying good riding stock." Shaking his head, he leveled an unwavering look at Rosalinda. "I tell you, Rosa, I hated that Tyler was hurt, but I was damned glad he got away from the Rocking P and that I left with him."

For long moments she thought about everything Gib had told her, and even though he hadn't given her details, he'd given her a sense of Tyler's life back in Texas. "What about now, Gib? You don't mind that Tyler has relegated you to cook?"

The question brought a grin back to the older man's face. "Naw. For a few years after we moved here I rode and worked out on the range. But the cold weather here in New Mexico gets brutal when you work outdoors all day long. Arthritis started working on my old injury, and after a while it hurt too much to sit for long hours in the saddle. Tyler put me to cooking. When I first started, the only thing I knew how to fix was bacon and eggs or making macaroni out of a box. We both suffered for a while."

Rosalinda smiled back at him. "Well, from the smell of things I think you've graduated into a true chef."

A door beyond Gib's left shoulder suddenly opened, and she looked up to see Tyler entering the room. He was smeared from head to toe with red mud.

"Rosa? How long have you been here?"

Before she could say a word, Gib said, "Long enough. Don't you know by now that it's not gentlemanly to keep a lady waitin'?"

Grimacing, Tyler pulled off his hat and tossed it toward a hall tree. It missed its mark, but he didn't notice as he'd already turned his attention to removing his muddy boots. While he tugged them off, Gib went over and plucked the hat from the floor, then hung it on an arm of the hall tree.

"Sorry I'm running late. It couldn't be helped," Tyler said. "A cow and calf got stuck in a bog hole. We finally had to use the tractor to pull them out. They appear to be okay, thank God. The men are fencing the bog off now."

"No need for apologies," Rosalinda told him. "Gib and I have been having a nice chat."

Tyler shot an amused glance at the other man. "Gib knows how to chat?"

She smiled at both men. "He did it very nicely with me."

Clearing his throat, Gib picked up Tyler's boots. "Get out of here before you smear mud all over the kitchen," he barked. "I'll have supper on the table in five minutes."

Tyler quickly strode out of the room, and Rosalinda rose to her feet. "Tell me what I can do to help."

The cook grinned. "I'll let you set the table. Come on and I'll show you."

From the kitchen, she followed Gib through an arched doorway and into a square-shaped room. A round pine table with matching chairs sat in the middle while a long, matching buffet rested along an inner wall. On the outer wall was a row of paned glass windows bare of curtains or drapes. But those furnishings would have only ruined the view of the backyard and the distant foothills of the rising mountains beyond.

Gib opened up a section of the buffet to expose a stack of dishes. "The silverware is in the top drawer and the dishes are here. Fix things like you want. Tyler doesn't care about fancy."

Gib left the room and Rosalinda went to work, placing the dishes and cutlery around the table. As she did, she couldn't help thinking the house was big and comfortable—just perfect for raising a large family. Children would love it here with all the livestock and wildlife and acres of land to explore. And so would a woman, she thought. The right woman.

And you're thinking you could be that right woman, Rosa? Just because the man kissed you a couple of times doesn't mean he wants to sign a marriage license. Dale gave you more than kisses. He promised to marry you, to love and protect you forever. But once Monique started applying pressure our love didn't matter and he crumbled. You expect Tyler to be any different?

"It's nearly dark. But if you look close you'll probably see a mule deer or two out there grazing on the foothills."

Realizing that Gib had walked into the room, she was thankful the cook believed she was appreciating the view instead of daydreaming about Tyler.

"The spring fawns are getting big now. You might spot some of them, too, following after their mothers."

The sound of Tyler's voice had her and Gib turning to see he'd entered the dining room. As he joined them at the table, she noticed he was dressed all in denim and his black hair was damp and slicked back from his face. At some point since she'd met him four days ago, he must have shaved at least once. Otherwise the dark stubble on his face would have been a lot longer. He was a man who either disliked razors or was extremely busy, she decided. Or could be he was unconcerned with his appearance. Either way, it hardly mattered. If he looked any sexier, she'd probably need to be resuscitated.

"There you are," Gib said to him. "'Bout time, too. Everything is ready."

"Good," Tyler said. "I hope you two are as hungry as I am."

Gib quickly scooped up one of the plates from the table and the silverware next to it. "My hip is aching a little. I'm going to eat in front of the TV in my room. You don't mind, do you, Rosa?"

Since she'd arrived this evening, Gib hadn't complained about having any pain to her. Was he deliberately leaving her alone with Tyler? It certainly looked that way.

"Not at all," she told him. "And since your hip is hurting, I'll do the cleaning up for you."

Gib's jaw dropped. "Naw. Guests don't do dishes."

She smiled at the cook, then turned it on Tyler. "I'm sure Tyler won't mind helping me. Will you?"

The stunned look on Tyler's face pulled a chuckle from Gib. "Now that sounds like a winnin' deal to me. Ty cleaning the kitchen."

Deciding he'd better get while the getting was good, Gib left the room and Rosalinda turned to Tyler. "Don't worry," she told him. "I'll take care of the dishes. It's the least I can do for this lovely meal he prepared."

For long moments, Tyler simply stared at her. Just when she thought he was going to chide her about the dishwashing duty, he stepped forward and pulled her into his arms.

Dazed, Rosalinda's head tilted back in an attempt to read his expression, but the only thing she could see was his dark face descending toward hers. And then suddenly he was kissing her with short, hungry sips that took her breath away.

By the time he was finished, she was practically gasping. "What was that?"

The lazy grin on his mouth made her wish he would kiss her all over again.

"Saying hello," he murmured. "And telling you how glad I am to see you again."

"Oh." The one word was all she could manage to say as her heart melted into a useless puddle at his feet.

It was going to be a night she would long remember, she decided. And she could only hope the memories she made with this man wouldn't soon turn into regrets.

Chapter Eight

To say that Tyler's greeting had caught Rosalinda off guard would be a huge understatement, but she tried her best to appear composed as he helped her into a dining chair.

"I see Gib has fixed pot roast. I hope you like it." After taking his seat, he handed her a bowl of tossed salad. "He's turned into a pretty good cook. Much better than I ever could become."

Once she'd helped herself to the salad, she reached for her water glass in hopes that the icy liquid would cool her throbbing lips. She wasn't a teenager by any means and she'd certainly been kissed before. But Tyler's were oh, so different. He tossed her upside down and made something inside her burn.

Trying to ignore the upheaval inside her, she said, "Gib told me about his injury and how he finally had to give up being in the saddle all day."

He shook a mixture of oil and vinegar over his salad. "Oh? Sounds like you two did have quite a chat."

"We talked a bit about the fire. And other things. He's a likable man and clearly devoted to you."

"I grew up tagging behind the man. We've always been like this." He held up two crossed fingers.

"I can tell he's proud that he once was a cowboy."

"Not was, Rosalinda. Gib still is a cowboy. He can still out-rope and out-ride the rest of the men on this ranch. Including me. The only difference is he'd be hurting like hell the day after. And I don't want that. Gib doesn't deserve to hurt." He cast her a sidelong glance. "Did he tell you how his accident happened?"

"Just that it involved a bucking horse during branding."

From her angle, she could see his right jaw tighten. "My father goaded Gib into riding Santana that day. Said if Gib was such a hand, he could handle the outlaw horse."

Questions were suddenly whirling through her mind. "I don't understand. Are you saying your father deliberately wanted Gib to be hurt?"

"I'll always believe it. See, Warren—that's my father—he was jealous of Gib in many ways. Because I'd always been so close to him. And he was dear to my mother, too."

She paused in ladling a portion of roast onto her plate and looked over at him. "Your mother? You mean—"

He grimaced. "No. They never had an affair if that's what you're thinking. Gib was just a good and kind friend to her. He understood how demanding Warren could be and he knew that Edie—my mom—often carried a heavy load. Gib would lend her an ear and empathize. That's all."

That would certainly go along with the demotion Warren Pickens had given Gib after the accident, she thought. "This is none of my business, but is your mother still there in your family home?"

"As far as I know. I only hear from her on occasions. Mostly by letter. Sometimes she calls from a pay phone. She doesn't want to leave traces that Dad might discover."

His remark was so stunning, she forgot about the food and leaned back in her chair to stare at him. "Are you serious?"

"Very." He passed her a bowl of baby carrots as though they were discussing the weather. "Don't get me wrong, Rosa. Dad would never harm Mom physically. But the verbal hell isn't good."

The day they'd ridden to the burn site, he'd talked about missing his mother. There had been a wistful note in his voice then and tonight it was back again. "So why does she stay? Why doesn't she come out here with you?"

His features were suddenly stoic. "I'm not sure. God knows there's no love between my parents anymore. But my brother and sister are still there."

His revelation caused her to stare at him. "You have siblings?"

"Trent. He's my twin. Connie is my sister."

Clearly something had happened to cause an iron wall to come between him and his family. But what? And why did it matter so much to her?

"That surprises me," she admitted. "Especially that you have a twin."

"Why? You can't imagine there being two like me in the world?"

There was a faint smile on his face, but she got the impression there was nothing amusing about his relationship with his brother.

"Are you two identical?"

His gaze dropped to his plate. "Not at all. But that's enough about the folks back in Texas. I'd like to hear what you've been doing. Are you making any progress on the case?"

He was changing the subject, but that was okay with

her. She wanted this night with him to be nice and easy, not fraught with emotion. And she understood, far more than he could possibly guess, that some things were just too hard to discuss with anyone.

"Well, two nights ago Hank and I had to work a shooting. We didn't wind that up until about two the next morning. The shooter is in jail, but expected to make bond. That fight was over a set of truck tires. People do idiotic things, but shooting at each other over truck tires is a new one for me. Yesterday we made a couple of domestic calls, but the remainder of the day we devoted to the fire case. Both the sheriff and undersheriff concurred with my idea about the suspect coming from the south. But that doesn't necessarily mean he works for the Chaparral. He or she could have been an outsider."

"Sheriff Hamilton phoned me yesterday," he said. "And he more or less implied the same thing to me. He didn't go into specific reasons, but he's crossed my men off the suspect list. That was a relief. But it still leaves me as leery as hell thinking that someone nearby might be out to ruin my land or livestock. I've decided to keep a guard on duty at the stables all night. That won't keep the cattle protected in the pasture, but it will make sure my best horses are safe."

She nodded. "That's a good idea. And I do hope you'll always keep your eyes open when you're out and about. Until we get to the bottom of this thing, we can't predict what might happen next. And I don't want anything to happen to you."

Her remark brought a soft light to his green eyes and he reached over and covered her hand with his. The gentle touch didn't match his rough and rugged appearance. But Rosalinda was learning there was much more to this man than what could merely be seen on the outside.

"It's nice to hear you're concerned for my safety," he murmured.

Her heart leaped into a hard, fast rhythm. "I'm a deputy. I'm concerned about everyone's safety."

"Hmm. I hope you don't go around kissing everyone like you kissed me a few minutes ago."

The teasing glint in his eye made it easy to give him a smile. "That was a sneaky thing to do. You caught me off guard."

"That was my plan."

She desperately wanted to turn her hand over and wrap her fingers around his. She wanted to behave as though she had every right to touch him in intimate and personal ways. And that scared her. Hank might be a pain in the neck at times, but he was right about one thing. She'd only known Tyler for a few short days. She shouldn't be feeling this close to the man. But she was. And she didn't know how to stop the strong, magnetic pull he seemed to have over her.

Clearing her throat, she awkwardly pulled her hand from his and reached for her water glass. After a long sip, she said, "You have a beautiful home, Tyler. Did you have the house built or was it here already?"

"Nothing was here except wild, beautiful mountains. I hired a contractor to do all the ground excavation and carpentry work. Before I got the house built I lived in an old rental in Alto and made the drive every day. Two years of that commute got old."

She glanced around her. "Well, the house certainly has plenty of space for one person."

The downward slant of his face made it impossible to read his thoughts. "Is that your way of asking if I built the house with plans to fill it with a family?"

A blush stung her cheeks. "Not exactly. But you must admit it looks that way. Otherwise, a small, one-bedroom cabin would have been enough living space for a bachelor."

He said, "Gib stays here in the house with me."

"Okay, make that a two-bedroom cabin."

He swallowed several bites of food before he finally spoke. "Look, Rosa, at the time I built the house I didn't know if I'd ever want a family. I only wanted a house that was nice and comfortable. That's all. There were no underlying plans or dreams. No romantic wishes."

If his words weren't enough to shower her with cold water, then the clipped sound to his voice should have turned her blood to ice and frozen any attraction she felt for the man. But oddly enough it worked exactly the opposite. Because something told her that beneath all those words he was hiding a heart full of loss and pain. And she knew exactly how that felt.

"I see. Well, I rent. So all I considered was the cost and whether the plumbing worked well," she said in an attempt to lighten the moment.

That brought his head up and he turned a wan smile on her. "Plumbing is an important consideration. You're a smart girl."

His comment should have made her feel good. Most women liked having a man appreciate her brain. But to be called smart only made Rosalinda feel like a fraud. Oh, most of the time she could convince herself that she had a head full of sense. But in reality, the past still often kicked sand in her face and called her stupid.

"Not really, Tyler. I mean, I try. But I—I've made my mistakes."

"Haven't we all?"

She let out a long breath. "Yes. I guess everyone makes them. Only some of us more than others."

Through the remainder of the meal, Tyler had trouble keeping his mind on his food. How could he think about anything with Rosalinda sitting only an arm's length away? Now and again he caught a whiff of her perfume and the evocative scent only added to the picture she made in that pink dress. Or was it coral? Either way, the color made her tan skin glow and tonight there was a lot of it for him to see. Her arms were bare and so was most of her chest. A tiny silver cross rested in the valley just where her breasts started a downward slope. In her ears silver hoops occasionally peeped through the dark hair lying upon her shoulders.

He'd been around nice-looking women before. He'd even been married to a sparkler. Rosalinda wasn't a glamour girl or drop-dead gorgeous. He couldn't quite label what made her so special. But he did know she was the essence of sexiness. And he was definitely feeling the effects. He wanted to have her in his arms, bury his face in her hair and let his hands explore her warm curves.

"I don't know about you, but I couldn't eat another bite."

Her voice interrupted his drifting thoughts and he looked over to see her resting her fork across her empty plate.

"I've had enough, too," he admitted.

She rose to her feet and began to gather the dirty dishes. Apparently, she'd meant it when she'd promised Gib to clean up for him. And though he liked the fact that she was willing to pitch right in and take care of the dishes, he'd much rather have her undivided attention.

"It isn't necessary for you to do this," he said. "I'll see to the mess later. Before I go to bed."

She shook her head. "I'm a woman who keeps her promises. And Gib has already shown me where most everything belongs. I'll have it done in no time."

Seeing he couldn't put her off, he rose to his feet and reached for a bowl of potatoes. "Okay. Let's get this over with so we can have coffee and dessert."

With both arms loaded with dishes, she started out of the room. Carrying the one bowl, Tyler followed a step behind her.

"You don't have to help," she tossed over her shoulder.

"I don't *have* to," he replied. "But I want to."

A few minutes later, Tyler realized she was right. With both of them working together it hadn't taken long to store away the leftovers and load the dirty dishes into the dishwasher.

While she'd finished the wiping up, Tyler put two cups of coffee and dessert plates holding slabs of white cake, topped with fluffy icing and fresh sliced peaches, onto a small tray.

When Rosalinda hung up her dish towel, she turned away from the sink and immediately spotted the tray he'd put together. "Tyler! I just told you I couldn't eat another bite," she gently scolded.

"Another bite or two won't hurt you. Let's go out to the back patio," he suggested. "I'll light the torches to keep the mosquitoes away."

"Outside sounds nice. I'll get the wrap I brought with me."

After retrieving a white lace shawl from the back of a kitchen chair, she wrapped it around her shoulders and followed him out the door.

One step down from a long back porch, a patio made of slab rock extended for twenty feet onto the green lawn. In one corner sat a small, glass-topped table and wrought-iron chairs. Nearby, a wicker chaise lounge and two matching rockers were shaded by the overhanging limbs of a huge pine.

Tyler carried the tray of food to the table, then went to work lighting two torches. A few feet away, Rosalinda stood at the edge of the patio and gazed out at the foothills.

"I wish I'd come out here earlier, before dark," she said wistfully. "The view is stunning. I don't know how you get any work done. If I lived here I'd just want to sit and stare and dream."

He carried one of the cakes and a coffee over to her. "After a while you'd get bored with that. You'd start wanting to see what was going on in those mountains."

"What is going on?"

He chuckled as he went to retrieve his own dessert from the tray. "If I didn't know better, I'd think you'd been a deputy for years."

Her soft laugh was as warm as the summer sun and as rich as the cake he was about to eat, Tyler couldn't help thinking. And the sound reminded him of just how long it had been since he'd heard laughter in his home, especially from a woman. The only females who'd ever been in his house had been wives or friends of cattle or horse buyers, and those occasions were few and far between.

"Sorry. Sometimes I start interrogating without even realizing it."

He came up to stand just behind her left shoulder. "Well, to answer your question, a lot is going on up there right now. The mountain slopes have grass on them now, so the cattle move higher and higher to find it. And along with the mama cows, the deer and other wildlife have new babies to feed and care for. Wildflowers are blooming and the streams are running fast from the snow melt."

"It sounds lovely," she replied.

Placing his free hand on her shoulder, he urged her slightly toward the northwest. "Remember the cabin I mentioned? If you can spot that patch of pines in the darkness, the cabin is there, nestled in a steep draw. You have to hike or ride a horse to get up there. When would you like to see it?"

"Mmm. Let me think about that," she said.

He took a bite of cake, then moved a fraction closer. "Not afraid to go up there with me, are you?"

Her head turned just enough to allow her to see his face. The sight of her lips made him forget the sugary frosting on his tongue.

"Afraid? Not at all. We've already made one trip into the woods together. I'm not worried about making a second one. I'm just not sure how my schedule will be for the next few days. It was difficult enough to get out here for supper."

"Then you're saying you will go?"

She glanced back toward the mountains. "Why are you trying to pin me down?" she murmured the question.

Why was he? Tyler asked himself. Heaven knows, he'd certainly not had any interest in taking a woman anywhere for any reason in a long, long time. Even when he'd been married to DeeDee he'd not spent a lot of time with her. She'd had her interests and he'd had his. But Rosalinda was very different from DeeDee. With her it wasn't constant chatter about me, me, me. With Rosalinda it was all about the people around her, including him. And that made him feel important and special. Something he'd never experienced with DeeDee or even his family.

He said, "It's nice to enjoy spending time with a woman again."

"Again?"

He sighed. "Damn it, Rosa, you got into the wrong branch of the law. You should have been a D.A."

Walking over to the table, she returned her cup and plate to the tray. "I can't help it," she said. "I'm a woman, too, you know. And women are curious creatures."

Downing the last bite of cake, he joined her at the table and deposited his plate next to hers. "What the hell, I would have told you sooner or later," he said with a grimace. "I guess tonight is just as good a time as any. I was referring to my ex-wife."

She turned to face him, and in the flickering torchlight, he could see her gaze delving into his. "You were married before you moved here?"

He nodded. “DeeDee was a tiny blonde with blue eyes and a bubbly personality. We were married for nearly five years.”

“She doesn’t sound like your type.”

He threw back his head and let out a mocking laugh. “Oh God, you sound just like my Dad now.”

“I’m sorry. I’ve not known you long enough to make that sort of assumption. I just meant that you seem like a no-nonsense sort of guy to me. I would have pictured your ex-wife being the practical sort.”

He moved a step away from her and stared out at the mountains. But the darkened landscape wasn’t what he was seeing in his mind. Instead, he was seeing DeeDee criticizing and taunting him. His father cursing and calling him a fool. And his brother standing back and just waiting for Tyler’s marriage to fall apart. For years now he’d tried to crush those memories and tell himself that none of that mattered anymore. But they always seemed to hang around and haunt him at the very worst of times.

He pushed out a heavy breath. “It was one of those opposites-attract things with us, I suppose. We met in college and I guess at that time her fun-loving personality was something I needed to help me get through the days of being away from the ranch. And, in a way, it was flattering to have her chasing me.”

Her eyes widened. “She chased you?”

“Go ahead,” he said in a voice heavy with sarcasm. “Tell me I’m not the type of man a woman would chase after, either.”

“It’s not that. I—” Frowning, she shook her head. “Please go on. What happened? Why did you divorce?”

“I asked myself that same question for years, Rosa. And I’m still not sure I know the answer. My father kept telling me that she was all wrong for me—that I was making all sorts of mistakes by giving her free rein. I wouldn’t listen. I was

just as obstinate as my dad. Anyway, in the beginning we had a pretty good marriage. But after a while she thought I was too much of a stuffed shirt for her, especially with Trent around. He kept her laughing."

"Your twin?"

"That's right. My twin. He stepped right in and did his best to make DeeDee happy."

As the meaning of his words sank in on her, disbelief filled her eyes as one hand crept up to her throat. "Did they—are you saying they had an affair?"

He swiped a hand over his face. Damn, but he'd not wanted to get into this tonight. But would tomorrow be any better? Or the day after that? No. There would never be a good time to talk about the very things he'd tried so hard to forget.

"I can't say for sure that they had an actual affair while we were married. But after we divorced, he didn't waste any time marrying her, if that tells you anything. I'd barely gotten out here to New Mexico when Mom got me the word that they'd flown out to Vegas and had a hasty wedding."

"What did you think? Or by then did you even care what they did?"

"No. My marriage to DeeDee was finished long before we ever divorced. And I guess you could say my relationship with my brother ended at that time, too."

"That's so awful, Tyler. I'm so sorry."

"Don't be. DeeDee isn't worth being sorry over. But my brother—that was different. When we were kids, the two of us were practically inseparable and we remained very close up until I went away to college."

"Trent didn't go to college with you?"

"No. Education never was high on his list of important goals. He wanted to stay home and help Dad run the ranch."

"College isn't for everyone," she reasoned. "Only two of my brothers went. The other two are doing fine without it."

"Well, I think that's when my brother and I drifted apart. I think he resented my desire to acquire a degree in ranch management. He thought I ought to stay home and build fences or brand cattle along with the rest of the crew. That was ranching to him. I wanted to learn how to make my ranch more profitable and to keep it that way. But even though we disagreed about that, I never once thought he would betray me by stealing my wife. But DeeDee had a way of manipulating people. She turned Trent and my father both against me."

"How did she manage to do that? Couldn't they see through her behavior?"

His laugh was harsh and mocking. "They were more focused on my behavior. They believed I was mean to DeeDee."

"Mean? Unless you've made a complete change in yourself I can't picture you being mean to a woman."

"Oh, I don't mean abusive. I simply tried to get her to behave more maturely. You see, I was always the serious, responsible twin while Trent was the fun-loving one of us. And now that I look back, maybe I was too serious for DeeDee. I wanted her to spend more time at home. I wanted her to have our children. She wanted to enjoy herself before she started all of that."

"And your brother and father agreed with her?"

"Of course Trent sided with her. They were two peas in a pod. As for Dad, he never liked DeeDee in the first place. Never wanted me to marry her. I honestly think he encouraged Trent to go after her."

"I don't understand. If Warren didn't want DeeDee in the family, why would he want his other son to show interest in her?"

"I don't think Dad ever thought Trent would go so far as to marry her. Though I can't be exactly sure about that. Once I filed for divorce, I sold my part of the family ranch and the cattle I owned and got the hell out of there. After that, I can't tell you what took place on the Rocking P. Mom just told me bits and pieces in her letters about DeeDee and Trent getting married."

"Are they still living on the ranch with your parents?"

"As far as I know."

"And your father? He doesn't care that you're not in his life?"

"He's an obstinate man, Rosalinda. He'd never admit he was wrong. Nor would he ever bend. From the time I was a small boy until I reached manhood, he tried to control every aspect of my life. Trent could do as he pleased, but I was to do as Warren Pickens ordered. When Dad started meddling in my marriage that was the last straw."

"Did you ever think he might have done those things out of love?"

Tyler snorted. "Love? I'm not sure Warren Pickens understands that word."

"Do you?"

"I used to think so. Now I'm not so sure." Moving up behind her, he slipped his arms around her waist and spoke against her ear. "I'm beginning to think I've never experienced the real thing. Not the kind between a man and a woman."

She turned in the circle of his arms and rested her palms against the middle of his chest. "There's a difference between love and sex, Tyler."

"I know. I've had the sex. Maybe someday I'll discover what the other is all about."

He could see the delicate arch of her throat working as she swallowed hard. "And what would you do, Tyler, if you did fall in love with a woman? You're bitter about marriage. I can hear that in your voice."

"I'm bitter about a lot of things that my family did to me.

But I like to think my life could be different. With the right woman by my side."

"Oh, Ty," she whispered, moving so close that the front of her body was touching his. "I dream of having the right man in my life. But my past is—"

"Everyone has some sort of past," he interrupted.

"Yes. Well, mine changed me."

"So did mine," he softly agreed. "But that was then and this is now." With his hands cradling her jaw, he drew her lips up to his and kissed her soft mouth until she was whimpering and his own need was rising.

"That kiss—it felt pretty special to me."

With fingertips pressed against her lips, she shook her head. "It's getting late," she murmured. "I think I'd better go."

He wasn't ready for this evening with her to end. At this very moment he wanted to kiss her until she was begging him to take her to bed, or he was begging her. But it was far too soon to press her for more. And way too soon for him to be wanting so much. He wasn't sure what was going on between them, but he couldn't just ignore this woman.

"All right. I'll walk you to your truck," he said.

"Thank you," she told him. "I'll get my purse from the kitchen."

Short minutes later, the two of them reached her truck. Tyler opened the driver's door for her and put a hand around her elbow to assist her into the cab. But she took him by surprise by suddenly turning to face him.

"I can't go without telling you how much I've enjoyed tonight," she said softly.

"So have I, Rosa. And that stuff about my family. You're the first to ever hear that."

A soft south wind rippled a strand of hair across her cheek, and he used his forefinger to tuck it behind her ear.

"I don't know what to say, Tyler."

She looked confused and anxious and he couldn't begin to understand why. "Don't say anything about that. Just tell me you'll go with me to the cabin. Or if you'd rather, I'll take you out on the town. To a movie or something."

She dropped her head. "I don't figure you're much of a town man. For you to offer to go to a movie—you must really want to spend time with me."

"I do," he said simply.

She released a long breath, then looked up at him and smiled. "Okay. I'm not much of a town person, either. I'd love to see the cabin. I'll call and let you know when I have a free day."

The joy that was rushing through him didn't make a lick of sense, but he cherished it more than if someone had filled his hand with pure gold.

"I'll be ready."

She leaned forward and kissed his cheek. "Good night, Tyler."

"Good night," he murmured.

He watched her drive away, until her taillights disappeared beyond the ranch yard, before he finally walked back to the house.

As soon as he entered the living room, he found Gib sitting in an armchair pretending to read a magazine.

"What the hell are you doing up?" Tyler asked.

Dropping the magazine, Gib rose to his feet and innocently flopped his arms at his side. "It's still early. Why wouldn't I be up?"

Tyler snorted. "Your hip was hurting. Remember?"

"And you're damned glad it was, ain't ya?"

Shaking his head, Tyler tried not to grin. "Okay, you old codger. I should thank you for letting me have Rosa all to myself."

A broad smile spread across Gib's face. "You're damned

right, you'd better thank me. She's a keeper. I hope you know that."

Tyler started out of the room only to have Gib follow after him.

"I've already figured that out without you having to tell me."

"Good," Gib said with a satisfied grunt. "Now you just got to figure a way to make her your girl."

Tyler whirled around so fast the other man nearly crashed into him.

"And what the hell if I do, Gib?" he challenged. "You think I could make her happy? Keep her happy?"

His jaw tight, Gib glared at him. "You let your old man bring you down once. You gonna let him do it again? Ten years, Tyler. Ten years. Don't you think it's been long enough for you to become your own man?"

Suddenly all the anger, dejection and hurt he'd endured from his family hit him like a sledgehammer and he was no longer seeing Gib, he was seeing his father and brother, feeling the cuts of their harsh, critical words.

"Get out of my sight," Tyler practically shouted at him. "Now!"

His face like a piece of stone, Gib stepped around him. "Gladly! And as far as I'm concerned you can get your own breakfast in the morning!"

The moment Tyler saw Gib limping away from him, he knew he was going to go after the man and apologize for his sudden outburst. He also knew that Gib would forgive him. Because the old man understood. Because Gib loved him even when he behaved like a bastard.

But could Rosalinda ever love him like that? Through the good times and the bad? Could she ever love him at all? He didn't know. But after tonight he realized he had to be man enough to find out.

Chapter Nine

Nearly a week after her dinner with Tyler, Rosalinda had just finished her self-defense class and was stuffing her dirty gym clothes into a duffel bag when a young woman who'd been a student for the past three weeks approached her. Her name was Daisy and no doubt she had the tiniest build of all the women in class. Light brown hair hung in fine wisps around her face and her blue eyes had a flat look that said her spirit had been broken long ago.

"Deputy Lightfoot? Could I speak with you for a minute? I promise I won't keep you long."

From the first night Rosalinda had spotted the young woman standing at the back of the room, she'd been drawn to her. And even though desperation had been written all over the woman, Rosalinda knew from experience that it was never a good thing to push anyone into talking about their personal problems. Everything worked better when it came from the person willingly. So Rosalinda had been biding her time, hoping and praying that Daisy would eventually come to her.

Smiling warmly, Rosalinda said, "Sure. I'm off duty tonight. I have plenty of time." Easing down on the locker bench, she patted the empty space beside her. "Why don't you sit down while I put on my boots?"

Sinking onto the edge of the bench, she said, "My name is Daisy Martell. I live off the highway toward Alto."

Rosalinda pulled on one brown cowboy boot and pulled the leg of her jean down over the shaft. "I saw your name on the roster, Daisy. Are you enjoying the class?"

Bending her head, she said in a quiet voice, "Yes. I'm not very good at the physical stuff yet. But I'm going to get that way. No matter how much I have to practice."

Rosalinda casually focused on pulling on her other boot. "You know, like I've said in class, being small doesn't mean you can't defend yourself. There are plenty of ways for you to stand up to whatever or whoever is threatening you."

Daisy's hands suddenly clamped together and she jerked her gaze to an empty corner of the room. "I didn't say I'd been threatened. I'm taking this class because—well, a woman never knows when someone might try to hurt her."

Rosalinda reached over and gently touched a fading bruise on Daisy's upper arm. "Would you like to join me at the Blue Mesa for a cup of coffee, Daisy? My treat."

This jerked the young woman's head up and she looked at Rosalinda with something next to panic in her eyes. "Oh—no. That's nice of you to ask. But I'd better not. My—well, someone might see me there. With you. And that would cause problems."

Since Rosalinda had come to the community center directly from work, she'd been wearing her deputy's uniform. And because she'd not bothered to pack a set of street clothes into her duffel, she'd put it back on after the class had ended.

Apparently, Daisy thought being seen with an officer of the law in a public place would be a huge risk for her.

Clasping Daisy's thin shoulder, she gave it a tight, reassuring squeeze. "It shouldn't be that way for you, Daisy. I think you know that without me having to tell you."

Biting down on her bottom lip, the young woman nodded glumly. "Yes. I know. I—I want things to get better. He makes promises. But then something bad happens and it starts all over again."

"It" meaning the cursing, hitting, threatening, Rosalinda thought sickly. As a law officer, Rosalinda had seen it firsthand on nearly a daily basis. As for herself, Dale had never been violent with her, but ultimately he'd caused her to be stalked, threatened and tormented until her life had been a living hell. It had been during those dark and lonely days that Rosalinda had learned abuse could be rendered in all sorts of ways, by man or woman. And once she'd managed to escape, she'd vowed to never allow it to happen again.

"Daisy. Trust me, I understand. You need to get out of this relationship you're in. It will only get worse."

"But—" She glanced over her shoulder as though she feared someone might be listening. "He'd come after me. And—"

Rosalinda interrupted with a shake of her head. "There are safe houses for women like you. We—Sheriff Hamilton and the rest—can help you disappear. Believe me. All you have to do is find the courage." She turned away from the woman long enough to dig a card from her duffel bag. "Here's my card with my personal number on it. Please take it. And call me anytime day or night."

Daisy looked at the card as though it were a snake. "I'd better not take it. I might not hide it good enough and then—" Shaking her head, she quickly jumped to her feet. "I'd better go. Thank you, Deputy Lightfoot."

Before she could scurry away, Rosalinda caught her by the arm and stuffed the card into her shoulder bag. "You'll find a place to hide the card. And I'm going to plan on hearing from you." She gave the fragile woman a gentle hug. "Good night, Daisy. And until I see you next week, take care of yourself."

Minutes later, as Rosalinda drove out of Ruidoso proper and east to the settlement of Ruidoso Downs, she wondered how Daisy managed to attend the self-defense classes. What sort of lies did she have to make up to be able to leave the house for an hour or two once a week?

It was a troublesome thought to Rosalinda, but once she let herself into her modest but cozy house, Rosalinda pushed the questions about Daisy aside. One thing she'd learned over the past few years was not to bring her job home with her. Otherwise, she'd be burned out before she reached the age of thirty.

Walking into the tiny kitchen, she poured herself a glass of cold water before pulling out her phone. She was sipping her drink and catching up on the numerous voice mails that had piled up during the day, when Tyler suddenly sounded in her ear.

"Gib told me you'd called, Rosa. Sorry I wasn't around to talk. If tomorrow is still good for the ride, I'll see you then. If you can't make it, let me know. I forgot to give you my cell number. So here it is."

As soon as he repeated the number, the message ended. For a moment Rosalinda considered playing it back just to hear his voice again. Oh, Lord, she couldn't be that smitten with the man. Could she?

Easing onto a chair at the kitchen table, Rosalinda sipped the water and rubbed fingertips across her taut forehead. Tomorrow would be a week since she'd had dinner with Tyler. Since he'd told her about his ex-wife and the break between him and his father and brother. It had been equally long since that heated kiss he'd placed upon her lips. And though his revelations about his family had dwelled in her thoughts, it had been the kiss that had haunted her the most. Just thinking about it now left her whole body hot and tingling. How was she ever going to make it through tomorrow without throwing her arms around him and begging him to make love to her?

If she had a brain at all, she would call him right now and tell him that she couldn't make it. That she had to work, or that she simply didn't feel up to making a horseback ride in the mountains. But none of that would be true. Tonight she'd told Daisy that she needed to make changes in her life. Well, the same could be said of herself, she thought. She didn't want to live the rest of her life alone. She wanted to be a wife and mother. She wanted to be everything a woman could be to a man. Somehow, someway, she had to find the courage to let Tyler into her life.

The next day Rosalinda arrived at the Pine Ridge Ranch shortly after lunch. Gib met her at the door and informed her that Tyler was down at the stables getting the horses ready for their ride.

She thanked him; then, rather than drive down the hillside to the ranch yard, she grabbed her bag and walked the distance over a well-padded trail.

As she passed a maze of cattle pens, she met three of the ranch hands she'd questioned that first day after the fire. Today they greeted her in a much more affable manner. Probably because she was out of uniform, she thought wryly. Or perhaps they'd learned the investigation was now concentrated on the Chaparral.

At the horse stables, she found Tyler in the saddling paddock, adjusting a breast collar on Inky, the black horse he'd ridden the other day. A few yards away, the paint, Moonpie, was already tacked up and tied to a cedar hitching post.

"So I'm riding Moonpie again?" she asked as she approached him and the horses.

The sound of her voice brought Tyler's head around and the smile he shot her filled her with unexpected pleasure. To see this man happy made her feel good in a way she didn't understand.

"You and Moonpie got along so well I decided to put you two together again."

"That's great. He's a honey horse."

Clearly amused by her remark, he stepped away from his mount to meet her. "Hmm. A honey horse. I don't think I've ever heard that equine description before."

Rosalinda chuckled. "That's my way of saying he's sweet."

She could feel Tyler's gaze wandering up and down her body and Rosalinda wondered if he'd been thinking about the kiss they'd shared on the patio. Had he remembered the way her lips had clung to his? The way her hands had explored his chest and locked over his shoulders? She'd not wanted to let him go or to give up the taste of his mouth. And something about the way he'd looked at her had said he'd not wanted to let her go, either.

If she'd not found the willpower to call an end to the evening, the two of them would've mostly likely ended up making love. Just the idea of being that connected to this man filled her with reckless excitement.

"You look like you're ready," he remarked. "Do you have everything with you that you'll need for the ride?"

"Right here." She patted her bag.

"I've put saddlebags on Moonpie. You can put whatever you need in them."

"Thanks."

She stepped over to the horse to transfer her things to the saddlebags when someone suddenly emerged from the tack room. Taking a second glance, Rosalinda saw that it was

Santo Garza, the wrangler she'd handcuffed and threatened to haul to jail. Seeing her, he walked over and, with a sheepish grin, reached a hand to her in greeting.

"Deputy Lightfoot, you're not here to arrest me today, are you?"

Smiling, Rosalinda shook his hand. "I'm off duty today, Santo. Call me Rosa. And I'm glad to see you're not still angry with me."

"Sorry about that. I was in a bad mood that day. The fire made me mad." The wrangler scuffed the ground with the toe of his boot. "Ty don't bother nobody. He don't deserve to have his land burned."

"I agree, Santo. Sheriff Hamilton has deputies patrolling the two ranches more frequently these days. And we're putting all our clues together. Hopefully we're going to catch the criminal before he does it again."

"I'll keep my eyes open, Miss Rosa. If I see anything suspicious I'll let you know. And this time it'll be the truth," he added with a chuckle.

"Thanks, Santo. I appreciate the help."

The other man went on his way and Tyler walked over to where she stood at Moonpie's side. As she watched him grow closer, Rosalinda's heart jumped into a quickstep. He was dressed in very faded jeans and a dark gray shirt with the sleeves rolled against his forearms. His lean body moved with lazy litheness, while the soft fabric of his clothing revealed well-honed muscles that came from years of strenuous outdoor labor.

"See, I told you Santo wouldn't hold a grudge over those handcuffs," he said.

"I'm glad." She reached for his hand and clasped it tightly. "And I hope you're not angry with me."

Beneath the brim of his gray hat, his brows formed a quizzical line. “Angry? Why would I be angry with you? You didn’t handcuff me.”

“I’m talking about last week. When we had dinner together. I left abruptly and I got the impression that you probably thought I was running away from you.”

“Weren’t you?” he asked softly.

Emotions tightened her throat. “Yes. In a way.”

Moving closer, he folded her hand between the two of his, and the warmth she drew from his touch was unlike any she’d experienced before.

“And what good did running get you?” he asked.

She dared to meet his gaze. “It kept us from doing something we might regret.”

“Like making love?” he asked huskily. “That’s not something I would have regretted, Rosa.”

His admission shook her. Because deep down she didn’t think she would regret giving herself to this man. It was the aftermath, and what it might bring, that worried her.

Glancing away from him and down the long shed rows, she watched a horse poke its head over a stall gate and nicker loudly.

“Well, for what it’s worth, I’ve missed you.” She brought her gaze back to his face. “Today is the first day I’ve had free in a long time. And I wouldn’t have had that if another deputy hadn’t offered to fill in for me.”

“Yesterday when Gib told me that you’d called, I was surprised. I figured you’d decided against making the ride to the cabin.”

With a faint shake of her head, she said, “I told you I would go. And I always try to keep my word.”

He touched a finger to her cheek. “I’m glad you kept it this time. And that you’re spending your free day with me.”

For a moment, the world seemed to stop and all she could think about was moving forward, pressing her body against his and seeking the delicious taste of his lips. But the ranch yard was full of busy cowboys and, behind her, Moonpie had begun to paw the dirt.

Suddenly she could feel the sexual spark between them, arcing like jagged lightning connecting two clouds. "I—uh—think he's saying we need to get going."

Clearing his throat, he dropped his hand and stepped back. "We do need to be on our way," he said, gesturing toward the paint. "Lead him up and I'll help you on."

When Rosalinda had first arrived at the ranch, the sky had been cloudless and the wind so faint that hardly a leaf stirred. But as she and Tyler rode west, then north into the mountains, heavy clouds began to roll in and the wind sang through the pines. Even so, the weather remained warm and as Tyler had predicted, the landscape grew ever more beautiful as the horses carefully picked their way up the mountain trail.

After about forty-five minutes, he motioned for her to follow him off the beaten path and onto a faint track that led into a thick stand of pines.

"If you're ready for a break, there's something over here I want to show you," he called back to her.

"I'll be right behind you," she assured him.

The trail through the trees was cushioned with a thick blanket of pine needles. The natural carpet muffled the clank of the horses' shoes, making the trek into the dense forest eerily quiet. But after a while a faint roaring sound interrupted the silence.

"I hear something," she called up to Tyler. "What is it?"

"You'll see. We're almost there."

A few more feet and the pines gave way to a small opening. Ten feet in front of them a bed of huge boulders rose high above their heads, blotting out the faint rays of light slanting through the fir trees.

"We'll have to leave our horses here," he told Rosalinda. "And walk through that crevice in the boulders."

He dismounted, then helped her down from the saddle. This time when her feet landed on the ground, her legs didn't feel quite as rubbery as they had the day they'd ridden to the burn site. But Tyler must have thought she needed supporting anyway. His hand remained firmly locked around hers as they walked through the narrow break in the rocks.

Once the two of them emerged on the other side of the boulders, Rosalinda gasped at the sight.

"A waterfall! And it's so huge! I didn't realize there could be this much water so high up on the mountain."

Standing at her side, he curved his arm against the back of her waist. Warmed by the connection, Rosalinda allowed her hip to rest against his.

"Later this summer there won't be as much water. And in the winter it freezes," he told her. "That's a sight to see. The whole thing turns to a wall of white ice."

"It must look like a winter wonderland when that happens. Can we get closer?" she asked.

"Only if you promise to keep hold of my hand."

"Cross my heart."

Tyler led her forward until she was close enough to peer over the edge of rock surrounding the falls. Some twenty feet below, the force of the water had cut a wide gash in the side of the mountain and formed a natural pond dammed by rocks, silt and underbrush. Aspens and desert willows grew nearby, shedding fragile shadows across the pool, while giving a playground to a flock of birds flitting from limb to limb. Although there was no other sign of wildlife at the moment, Rosalinda could easily see this place as a watering hole for deer and bears and possibly even mountain lions.

"Do your cattle ever water here?" she asked curiously. "Or is it too rough and wild for them?"

"They do. Although they aren't in this area right now. The men have moved them over to the eastern slopes."

"So how far is it to the cabin from here?"

Easing her back from the rock ledge, he pointed in a northwesterly direction. "Up there. About ten more minutes."

To reach their destination, they had to ride up above the falls, then over for a quarter more of a mile. By then, they'd left the dense forest of pines and instead twisted juniper and huge clumps of sage began to emerge between scrubby piñon trees. When they finally rode to the top of a barren crest, a narrow canyon lay before them. To one side of the deep crevice, a small cabin made of chinked logs sat precariously on the steep mountainside.

"There it is," Tyler announced. "What do you think?"

Standing up in her stirrups, Rosalinda peered at the sight before her. "It looks like something out of a Western movie. A place bandits would use to hole up with their stolen gold."

"Funny that you should mention gold. That's the reason the cabin is here. An old prospector built it to live in while he worked his mine."

"There's a mine around here?"

"Not far from the cabin. Come on and I'll show you."

At the cabin they dismounted and Tyler quickly eased the girths on Inky and Moonpie and, after removing their saddlebags, turned the horses loose in a small grassy area so the animals could graze.

"Do you want to see the mine first or the inside of the cabin?" he asked.

Chuckling, she rubbed the front of her weary thighs. "I think we'd better look the mine over first. Otherwise, if I sit down I might never get back up."

After drinking from the bottled water packed in their saddlebags, Tyler guided her to a spot about thirty feet up and behind the cabin. There, a small entrance in the side of the mountain was framed with rotted timbers. An X of newer-looking boards had been nailed across the opening to prevent cattle or curious little calves from exploring the dangerous cavern.

"So what was supposedly mined here?" Rosalinda asked as she poked at the fine gravel spilling out from the doorway. The small rocks were a strange orange and yellow color that didn't match the big boulders lying around on the ground.

"I'm not sure. Could've been silver or gold. I've heard stories of both. You know that Quint did find a very lucrative gold deposit on his ranch over by Fort Stanton?"

"Yes. I've heard Brady speak of the Golden Spur Mine. Last I heard they were still hauling ore from it." She gestured toward the small opening. "This must've been some guy trying to strike it on his own. Wonder if he ever found anything?"

"I doubt it. Otherwise, he would've stuck around and expanded the dig."

Turning away from the mine opening, she stared southward. From this point, the view was more open. She could even glimpse a slither of the Rio Bonito winding its way across a small valley. "He stuck around long enough to build a house," Rosalinda pointed out. "Could be he found something more important than gold or silver here." Maybe he'd found a woman in town and decided marrying her and having a family was more important than gold, she thought.

She turned her gaze on him. "You've never thought about having a geologist test this area?"

He shook his head. "I want to keep my peace of mind, Rosa, not wreck it worrying about discovering the mother lode."

So he wasn't interested in becoming rich. At least, not rich in precious metals. But what about love? She'd thought a lot about the things he'd told her of his life in Texas and what he'd gone through with his ex-wife and family. He'd basically lost his whole family. Would he ever want to try and patch it back together? Ever want a family of his own?

He'd probably resent those questions, she thought. And she had no right asking them. Not when she was still keeping her past with Dale a secret.

Reaching for her arm, he said, "Let's go back to the cabin. Gib packed us some snacks."

"Sounds good," she agreed.

As they descended the steep ground, she focused her thoughts to the present. "Is the trail we rode here to the cabin the only way to get here? I mean, obviously it can be hiked from any direction, but I was talking about another trail that a horse or even a four-wheeler could travel."

"There's another trail just west of here. It actually runs into a road that travels over Chaparral land. In fact, that's the road where Alexa, Quint's sister, was kidnapped by cattle rustlers a few years ago. It caused quite a stir—brought all the family together. And her husband—the Texas Ranger—was the one who found her."

"Hmm. That's interesting."

"Why? What are you thinking?"

"Just wondering if this place might be connected to the fire in any way? How far is it from here to the cliff where the fire was set?"

"Oh, as the crow flies probably a half mile," he said thoughtfully. "But it's rough going. The road west of here on Chaparral land would give a person a lot smoother access to the cliff. A bit more distance, though."

"Well, it was just a thought." She looked at him and smiled. "But that's enough about that. I don't want to spend my day off going over clues."

"Neither do I," he agreed.

Back at the cabin, Rosalinda followed Tyler onto the small planked porch, then through a thick, wooden door.

"With the windows all shut, it's pitch-black in here," he warned. "Give me a moment and I'll get some light."

While she waited in the doorway, he unlatched the heavy wooden shutters and shoved them open. As the muted daylight streamed through the square openings Rosalinda looked curiously around the room.

A small square table sat in the middle of the board floor. On the back wall were a row of shelves made of rough lumber, along with a small counter that held a granite wash pan and galvanized water pail. To the right of the table, a crude bedstead had been built into a corner. Rosalinda was surprised to see it was made up with a patchwork quilt and two pillows in clean white cases. A few feet down from the bed, a rock fireplace stretched across another corner.

"My ranch hands use this old place during the hunting season. They stock it up with food and lay in some firewood for cold weather. Right now it's pretty dusty and empty."

Intrigued by the sturdy structure, Rosalinda stepped farther into the room. "I like it. It's very rustic, but very charming. Do you ever stay here overnight?"

"I have. But it's been a while. For the first year or two after I purchased this land I used to come up here just to be alone. I'd sit on the porch and stare down at the valley and ask myself if I'd done the right thing."

"The right thing about what?" She walked over to the fireplace and trailed her fingers over the rough mantle. What sort of man had built this cabin? she wondered. A man like Tyler? One driven and determined to make it on his own? One thing was for sure, both men had been adventurous.

When he didn't answer immediately, she glanced around to see him shrugging one shoulder.

He said, "Buying this piece of land. Some of the so-called

cattlemen around here warned me that I'd never be able to run Herefords on it—swore there were too many mountains and not enough meadows. But I've proved them wrong. Them and a few more folks, I imagine."

"You're talking about your family now?"

Nodding, he lifted the globe from the lamp and struck a match. Once the wick began to burn, he adjusted the flame and returned the globe. "I don't expect my father or brother ever expected me to survive on my own. They both believed I relied on my brain too much instead of my back."

"I always believed a person had to rely on both to succeed." She walked over to him. "Do you think your family knows you've made a success of this ranch?"

"I've told my mom that I'm doing okay for myself. She might tell my sister a few things. But not the menfolk."

She shook her head in disbelief. "I don't understand. What would happen if your mother told them she'd contacted you? So what? You're her son. She has that right. It sounds like she's more of a possession than a wife."

He grimaced. "She's—well, submissive. And she keeps her mouth shut to keep the peace. But I still talk to a few old friends back in Texas. I imagine they've passed information along to the family. But that hardly matters. I don't have anything to prove to my dad or my brother anymore. And my sister has her own life to worry about."

He suddenly reached for her, and as his hands came around her shoulders, she went willingly into his arms. "But you, Rosa, I do have something to prove to you."

Her breath lodged in her throat as his hands slid against her back and drew her body snug against the front of his. His sinewy muscles were as hard as a rock and the heat radiating from his body torched her with excitement. "Like what?" she asked teasingly.

His head bent and his lips hovered temptingly over hers.

"Like proving how much I want you in my arms. Not just for a few minutes, but for as long as you'll stay."

A shaky breath rushed out of her. "Tyler—I—this is—I think I need some air."

He didn't try to stop her as she slipped out of his arms and once she was past the open doorway, she didn't stop until she was off the porch and walking down the slope of the mountain. By the time she reached a grassy knoll shaded by a copse of aspens, the fresh air had helped to untangle the jumbled thoughts in her head. As she leaned against one of the white tree trunks, it dawned on her that the uncertainty she'd experienced back in the cabin had nothing to do with Tyler. She'd not been running from him. She'd been running from her past.

Drawing in a deep, cleansing breath, she was trying to figure out how to explain herself to Tyler when she heard the snap of a twig behind her and realized he'd followed her. Then, seconds later, his hands came gently down on the back of her shoulders.

"Rosa, what's wrong?" he asked gently. "You aren't afraid of me, are you?"

She swallowed as a surge of emotions thickened her throat. "Yes, I am. But not in the way you're thinking." Turning, she faced him. "I'm afraid of the way you make me feel."

"And how do I make you feel?"

Resting her palms against his chest, she was stunned at how right it felt, how the doubts and questions suddenly fell aside. "When I decided to come with you on this ride I think deep down I knew this might happen. And deep down I realized that I wanted it to."

"That was a funny way of showing it. Running from me like that."

Her hands slid up his chest and latched over the top of his

shoulders. "I needed a moment to think, Ty. You know, wanting something doesn't necessarily make it right."

His lips twisting to a wry smile, he murmured, "Doesn't make it wrong, either."

Rosalinda looked into his green eyes and suddenly she remembered the first morning she'd met him. The iciness in his eyes had haunted her. But that coldness was gone now and thinking she'd brought warmth back to his life made her happy. As happy as anything had ever made her.

Lifting a hand, she gently brushed her fingers against the ridge of his cheekbone. "Make love to me, Ty."

But would it be love or sex? As his lips came roughly down on hers, Rosalinda told herself that right now it didn't matter. She wanted him and he wanted her. And this time she wasn't going to run.

Chapter Ten

His hands came up to clasp her face and he held her like that for long moments, his lips prodding, urging her to give him more and more.

When their tongues mated and helpless moans sounded in her throat, he began to ease her down onto the bed of grass beneath their feet. The movement caused their mouths to break apart and Rosalinda used the moment to regain her breath. But the reprieve was short-lived. As soon as he had her lying next to him, his lips found a spot at the side of her neck and his hands molded around her breasts.

Sweet desire plunged through her body and drove a flare of heat straight to the very core of her. The intensity of it left her senses spinning and her hands clinging helplessly to his shoulders.

"Rosa, Rosa." He whispered her name as his lips made magic circles over her cheeks, nose and chin. "When I first saw you, something hit me. I don't know what it was. But I never expected to feel like this—to want you so much."

His breath against her face was so utterly masculine it seeped into her skin like an intoxicating fog and sent her senses spinning wildly. She thrust her fingers into his hair as her head tilted back to give him even more access to the line of her throat. “Ever since you kissed me, I—oh, Ty—I think you’ve made me a little crazy.”

“Crazy. Wonderful. I think I’m dreaming,” he said against her skin. “But it feels too good—too real to be a dream.”

His fingers went to work on the buttons of her shirt and once the pieces of fabric parted, his mouth sought the flesh between the cups of her bra. The intimate touch shot a buzz of sensation up and down her body and drew tiny moans of pleasure from her throat.

“We could go back to the cabin,” he whispered the suggestion. “The bed would be softer for you.”

“I don’t need soft,” she assured him. “It’s beautiful here on the grass with the leaves above us.”

“Mmm. And it’s even more beautiful with you in my arms.”

Quickly, he tugged her to a sitting position so that he could remove her shirt and release the hooks at the back of her bra. Once he’d eased the blue lace away from her breasts and exposed them to his hungry gaze, she’d expected to feel self-conscious, especially since they were outside in broad daylight. Instead, she felt empowered by the reverent glow in his eyes. And the desperate ache to have his mouth upon her breasts caused her upper body to arch instinctively toward his.

Responding to her invitation, he laved one breast with his tongue. At the same time, she pushed her hands up his sides until she found an opening in his shirt. Wantonly, she pulled the snaps apart, slipped her hands inside and slid them brazenly across his chest.

The exploration of her fingers caused his head to lift,

and with his hands on her shoulders, he slowly lowered her back against the grass. Once they were lying side by side, he pulled her close against him, his mouth feeding on hers while his fingers explored her breasts, the faint ridges along her rib cage and the smooth valley around her belly button.

By now her breaths were coming in tiny sups with hardly enough oxygen to replenish her starved lungs. It wasn't right to want a man this much. No. This desire for him was so deep, so shattering that it had to be dangerous. But she was beyond caring about the danger now.

When his fingers finally reached for the zipper on her jeans, he pulled his head back and met her drowsy gaze.

"Rosa, if this is too much for you—if you want to stop now—tell me," he urged, his voice raw with tightly reined emotions. "I don't want this to be something you'll regret."

Her head shook back and forth against the thin mattress. "No regrets, Ty. No matter what happens later."

He closed his eyes and she felt something stir in the middle of her chest as she watched the muscles in his throat work to swallow. He might show a tough veneer to everybody else, but he was a different person with her. He was a bit more open and vulnerable, and the gentle touch of his hands could only have been guided by a softness within him. And it was that softness that made her want to wrap her arms around him and never let go.

Pressing his cheek against hers, he pushed his fingers into her hair and stroked the dark strands away from her face. "How did I ever find you?" he asked, his voice full of wonder. "I was so angry about the fire. But now—the damned thing brought us together. Does that make sense?"

"Maybe it was meant for us to start a fire of our own," she teased.

Groaning, he eased back from her and finished manipulating the zipper. Once he'd tugged off her boots, he slipped her jeans and panties over her hips. Tossing the garments aside, he looked down at her, and the smoldering haze in his green eyes shattered what little composure she had left.

With desire pounding inside her, she scrambled to a sitting position and reached for the front of his jeans. As she dealt with the buttoned fly, the sharp intake of his breath joined the sound of blood throbbing in her ears.

"Let me do this," he said urgently. "Or I'm going to be the one going up in flames."

Leaning back on her elbows, she watched him shed his boots and jeans, then lastly a pair of navy blue boxers. The sight of his erection caused her breath to catch in her throat and her fingers to curl into the blades of grass. The need to feel him inside of her was burning her mind and it was all she could do to keep from grabbing and pulling him close to her.

"I think I should tell you I didn't bring any protection with me," he said as he eased himself over her. "It hadn't been a plan to seduce you. I just wanted to share this special place with you. If I'd thought there had been a chance..."

She curled her arms around his waist and tugged him against her. "It wasn't my intention to seduce you, either. But this was meant to happen, Ty. Somewhere. Somehow. The time just happened to be now."

His eyes delved into hers. "Is there a possibility you might get pregnant?"

"I'm not sure I'd stop this even if there was a chance of me having your baby," she admitted in a rushed whisper. "But not to worry. I'm protected and healthy."

"So am I," he murmured against her lips. "Healthy, that is. And I want you, Rosa, more than I've ever wanted anything."

"Oh, Ty, make love to me. That's all I want."

There was no need to repeat her plea. In the blink of an eye, he rolled her onto her back and his hand sought the juncture between her thighs.

The instant his finger slid into her wet folds, a guttural sound of pleasure rolled from deep within in her throat. At the same time his head bent to her breasts and while his fingers teased her feminine core, his lips tormented one nipple, then the other.

Desire hummed through her until every particle in her body was throbbing and aching for relief. Finally, when she began to writhe beneath him, he removed his hand and used his knee to part her thighs even wider.

Gripping his buttocks, she urged his hips down to hers and he joined their bodies with one smooth thrust.

Overwhelmed with sensations, she could do little more than breathe his name. "Ty. Oh, Ty."

"Rosa. Touch me. Love me. Before I break apart."

His choked plea only added to the sweet ache his body was building in hers, and as they began to move in unison, she closed her eyes and let his driving thrust carry her away.

As Rosalinda's heated softness enveloped Tyler, he lost all sense of his surroundings. All sense of everything but the woman in his arms. Over and over he took what his body was craving, yet at the same time he hoped he was giving something back to her. He wanted to fill her with the same sort of pleasure that was consuming him.

Behind them, sunlight streamed over the crest of the mountain. It cast streaks of golden color across Rosalinda's lovely face, and Tyler thought how the prospector might not have found his treasure here, but he'd found his, right here in his arms.

The realization lanced through him like a sudden strike of lightning and the power of it sent his senses flying, his body into an even more frantic pace. Beneath him, Rosalinda matched his urgent lunges while her lips and hands touched him in places that drove him ever higher.

From somewhere far away, he could hear her choking out

his name, begging him for release and then suddenly stars exploded behind his closed eyes and he gripped Rosalinda as he drove deep into her for one last time.

Awareness crept back to Tyler in whirling fragments. The bright afternoon sun slanting across the ground. The birdsong in the branches above them and Rosalinda's warm breath brushing against the side of his neck. Something was holding him down and after dragging in another lungful of oxygen, he realized it was Rosalinda's fingers gripping his shoulder blades.

His cheek was pillowed against the curtain of her hair. It smelled like lilac and sunshine while, beneath him, her skin felt like damp silk.

Slowly, her hold on his shoulders relaxed and her hands fell limply to their bed of grass. He needed to move. To relieve her of his weight. But he could hardly bring himself to break the connection of their bodies. It was paradise. She was paradise.

With a reluctant groan, he forced himself to roll away from her, then reached for his shirt and folded into a makeshift pillow. As he tucked it beneath her head, her eyelids lifted and she looked at him with a drowsy sweetness that melted his insides.

"Thank you," she murmured.

A teasing grin curved his lips. "For the pillow?"

She sighed. "For everything."

Stretching out beside her, he rested a hand upon her flat belly and nestled his head in the curve of her shoulder.

I'm not sure I'd stop this even if there was a chance of me having your baby.

Even as he'd made love to her, those words had rolled over and over in Tyler's head. Had she really meant them? Would she ever be willing to give him that much of herself? Did he really want that much from her? The questions scared him, but it was time he started facing them.

"No, Rosa. I'm the one who's thankful." His throat tight with emotions, he pressed a kiss on the throbbing vein at the base of her neck. "Thankful that you've made me feel like a man again."

She laid her hand upon his cheek. "Ty, I can't believe you ever lost that feeling. You're a man who could have most any woman you want."

He picked up a strand of her hair and rolled the silkiness between the pads of his fingers. "That's just it, Rosa. I haven't met any woman that I've really wanted. Until you. Until now."

For long moments she was silent and then she slid her arm around his waist and rolled toward him. With her face nestled close to his, she said, "What just happened between us…it was amazing. But do you think all of this might be happening too fast?"

Her voice wavered with uncertainty, but that didn't surprise him. His own concerns were roiling around in his head, trying to put a damper on the afterglow of their lovemaking. But he wasn't going to allow his or her worries to take over. This thing that was sprouting between them needed to be nurtured and protected. Not crushed with doubts.

"Would slowing things down make things any better for us?" he asked in return.

She gazed at him, her eyes soft and hopeful. "Probably not. But where do we go from here?"

He pressed his lips against her forehead. "We'll figure that out together," he promised.

Sighing, she edged her body closer to his. "Can we stay here like this for a few more minutes?"

He wrapped his arm around her. "I couldn't move if I tried."

* * *

The sun was down and twilight was settling over the ranch yard by the time Tyler and Rosalinda returned to the stables. Santo met them at the saddling paddock and immediately took over the task of caring for the horses.

Back at the house they found a note from Gib lying on the countertop.

Supper is in the warming tray of the range. Big poker game planned. I'll be staying at the bunkhouse tonight with the boys.

"Poker game? Gib never cared about card playing," Tyler remarked. "I think my cook has deliberately left us alone again."

Drawing her close, he rested his forehead against hers. "Let's get cleaned up and eat. I don't know about you, but I'm starved. You don't have to go home early tonight, do you?"

"Not unless I'm called out on an emergency."

"Great. Then let's hope everyone in the county is on their best behavior tonight."

Much later, after their meal, they had coffee and dessert on the front porch, where a massive view of the southern sky spread before them and stars twinkled upon the distant mountain range.

Out in the lawn, frogs and crickets sang. Farther down the hill, horses whinnied back and forth to each other while cows occasionally bawled to their calves. Other than those peaceful sounds, the night was incredibly quiet.

"When I'm home, I don't much like the quietness. But up here it's different," she mused aloud. "It's like a comforting blanket."

As she sat close beside him on a wicker love seat, his arm was around her shoulder and now and then his fingers played with the ends of her hair. She could easily picture herself with this man even after they'd grown old and feeble. But she couldn't let herself start thinking and hoping now. It was too soon. Their relationship had just now begun.

"With your job you probably don't have much time to spend at home," he remarked.

"Since I've become a deputy, I've mostly volunteered to work extra duty," she confessed. "I'd rather be busy learning my trade than home alone thinking about things I'd rather forget."

He turned his head toward hers and she could feel his curious gaze sliding over her profile. Like a finger tracing a shadow on the wall. It was a slow, evocative study that shook her almost as much as the touch of his hand.

"We all have things we'd like to forget, Rosa. But I can't see you having that many bad memories."

His remark caused her insides to stiffen. "You can't imagine."

Her voice sounded strangled to her own ears and she wished she'd not brought up her past. But Tyler had already revealed so much about himself. It was only right that she open herself to him. But no one liked to admit to being a fool. And more than anything, she wanted Tyler to think of her as smart and strong. She wanted him to see her as much more than that bubbly blonde who'd disillusioned him and caused him to turn away from women.

"I can imagine lots of things, Rosa. Don't be embarrassed to tell me that some guy broke your heart. Isn't that what happened? A young woman as attractive as you couldn't have gone through half of her twenties without falling in love."

His last word pulled a cynical snort from her. "I only thought I was in love, Tyler. Now that I look back, I think I was obsessed with the idea of having someone to plan my future with more than someone to love."

He shifted so that he was facing her. "So there was someone important in your life."

"When I lived in Gallop," she replied, "I had moved off our family farm to start college and was just beginning to work toward a degree in education when I met Dale. We were together for several months before we finally got engaged. That's when all the trouble started."

"You found out he was cheating on you."

Shaking her head, she said, "If only it had been that simple. You see, Dale wasn't cheating. In fact, in the beginning I truly think he cared about me. My parents liked him. My whole family was happy for me. Everyone believed he would make a good, caring husband. Then about the time we announced our engagement, the trouble started and everything began to spin out of control."

Confusion wrinkled his brow. "What sort of trouble?"

She gazed out at the dark lawn stretching away from the porch. Here on the Pine Ridge Ranch, her ordeal with Dale seemed almost dreamlike, but four years ago it had been a living nightmare. "The stalking. The threats. The weeks of wondering who would be killed first. Me or Dale."

Incredulous, he stared at her. "Killed?"

Feeling too restless to sit still, she rose from the love seat and walked to the edge of the porch. Leaning against the arched rockwork that supported the roof, she said, "You see, when I first started dating Dale he'd recently ended a long-term relationship with Monique. I didn't know the woman, but from what he explained, the two of them were poison for each other and he wanted to put the affair far behind him."

"And you believed him."

Jerking her head around, she stared at him over her shoulder. "Yes. He meant it—at the time. He just wasn't strong enough to stick with it. Not after Monique started harassing me with threatening phone calls, following me, leaving nasty notes on my car windshield, breaking into my apartment. I could go on and on. But mostly it's all too horrific to repeat."

He left the cushioned seat and came to stand behind her. "I've heard of men doing that sort of thing, Rosa. But not a woman. How did you deal with her?"

"Hmm. At first it was hard to accept that any of it was happening. And then I thought—well, I can handle this. I figured Monique was just a sore loser and after a while she'd move on and leave us alone. But I was wrong. Her behavior grew more bizarre and dangerous. Not only toward me, but toward Dale, also. At first we tried to deal with the problems on our own. But when she confronted me physically I was forced to go to the police and get a restraining order from the judge."

"Did that help?"

With a cynical little laugh, she shoved her hair back from her face. "I'm now a law officer and I respect everything our job stands for. But we can't provide 'round-the-clock protection for every citizen in Lincoln County. It's not possible. It was the same in McKinley County. Eventually, one night, when I was driving home from my family's farm, Monique drove up on my back bumper and tried to ram me. I lost control of my car and it careened off the highway. It landed upside down and for a while I was pinned inside the wreckage."

"My God! What did it do to you?"

"Broke my arm just above my wrist and cracked a few ribs. But mentally I was more wrecked than my car."

"So that must have put an end to Monique's mischief, right? She was arrested?"

"You would have thought so. But the incident occurred on a lonely stretch of highway. Without witnesses, I had no way of proving Monique's involvement. But by then I didn't care if the woman was punished. I just wanted out and away from it all."

"What about Dale? If he loved you and you were planning to be married—"

Turning, she reached for his hand and squeezed it tightly. "Even before the wreck Dale had already started to crumble. More and more he'd started giving in to Monique's demands, agreeing to meet her to talk. To reason with her, or so he'd always said, because he wanted to keep her from harming me."

"Sure," he said sardonically. "Well, the man was either very weak or very stupid. That's all I can say."

"Both, I think. But I was more stupid, Ty. I should have gotten out as soon as the mess with Monique started. Instead, I wanted to believe Dale was a strong, capable man. I wanted to cling to the dream I had of marrying and having a family."

"So what happened with you and Dale after the accident?"

"I think deep down he was relieved when I returned his engagement ring. By then, both of us had realized our relationship had collapsed. After that, I left town and moved down here to live in Mescalero on the Apache Reservation."

"You didn't want to return to your family home?"

She shook her head. "Monique had frequently threatened to harm my family, too. I didn't want to take any chances that she might carry them out. Besides, I was a grown woman. It was time for me to stand on my own two feet and support myself. And I suppose I was a bit like you. I wanted to start over in a fresh new place. As for Dale and Monique, my family informed me later that he'd been seen around town with her. So apparently he went back to that poisonous relationship. He took the easy route of dealing with a bad situation."

"Does that bother you now?"

"No. What bothers me is the bad judgment I used. That's why—well, since all of that happened with Dale I've not let myself get involved with any man. Until you."

Tugging on her hand, he pulled her close against him and Rosalinda buried her face against his shoulder.

"Rosa, my sweet, I'm so sorry you had to go through all that. But it wasn't your fault. You weren't stupid to want things to work for you and Dale."

Tilting her head back, she looked at him. "But I should have realized it was hopeless. I was an idiot for hanging on until I was nearly killed."

"Yes. And I should've realized it was hopeless with DeeDee, too. I should have walked away from her long before my family was ripped apart. I think—well, failure is a hard thing to accept, Rosa. I didn't want to let go and admit to it any more than you did."

There was nothing critical in his expression, only compassion, and in that moment Rosalinda knew that no matter what happened in the future, this man was changing her life.

"I told Sheriff Hamilton and Undersheriff Donovan about the ordeal back in Gallop. Because as my bosses, I thought they deserved to know. Especially if the woman ever got it in her head to cause more trouble for me. That would ultimately reflect upon the sheriff's department."

"That won't happen. She's won her prize."

"Well, I just wanted you to know that you're the only other person I've told about it. I think—" She cradled her hands around his face. "After this afternoon—it was your right to know."

His arms tightened around her shoulders. "Rosa, I think tonight we both need to forget about our past mistakes. Right now it's enough that we're together. Isn't it?"

It wasn't enough for Rosalinda. This man was beginning to take up residency in her heart. It would be nice to hear that she was becoming special to him, that he wanted more from her than just a heated affair. But that would be expecting too much, too soon from him, she told herself.

Dropping her hands from his face, she sighed. "Yes. I suppose so."

He must have picked up on the dejected tone in her voice because he suddenly frowned. "I guess this is where a gentleman would be making promises to you, Rosa. And I wish I could. But I—"

"No," she swiftly interrupted. "I don't expect promises right now, Ty. This thing between us has just started. We both need more time to let it grow—to learn each other better."

"And tonight is the perfect time for us to start learning," he murmured huskily.

Lifting her into his arms, he carried her into the house and straight to his bedroom. And as he made love to her a second time, she wondered how long she could keep holding her heart together. How long would it be before he held it and her in the palm of his hand?

Chapter Eleven

Five days later, she and Hank were still going full steam on the arson case and as they climbed back into their truck to leave the Chaparral Ranch, Hank tapped the notebook he'd stuffed into his shirt pocket.

"We're getting somewhere now, Rosa. The arsonist has to be a person working on this ranch."

He started the engine and the air-conditioning vents on the dashboard immediately began to blow. Rosa leaned forward to let the air cool her face. It had been a hot day and she and Hank had spent most of the afternoon milling around the barns and feedlots on the big ranch. Both of them had interviewed and questioned several ranch employees for the first, second and third times since the fire had happened three weeks ago.

"We don't have anything concrete. But I do agree with you," Rosalinda told him. "The cowboy named Guy said that two fuel cans were always kept in the tractor shed, but at some point during the day of the fire he'd noticed them missing."

Frowning thoughtfully, Hank backed the truck away from the barn and began driving out of the huge ranch yard. "Yes. But I questioned him the very first day after the fire. Why didn't he tell me that from the very beginning? I'm wondering if he decided to speak up now to make it appear like he was being helpful or he could be trying to shed suspicion on someone else."

"Everyone was shaken after the fire, Hank. It's only natural that people weren't recollecting everything that happened that day. And then there's Saul. He admitted to filling up two plastic jugs with gasoline earlier that day. To use in a lawn tractor and weed eater. Or so he said."

"Yeah. Well, he had to admit to that. Everyone who uses the gas and diesel tanks on the ranch has to sign a log and register the amount they've pumped out. Anyway, I believe that old guy. He's worked on the ranch for years. And he moves so slow you can see the lice falling off him."

"Hank! The man doesn't have lice!" she scolded.

Hank chuckled. "I meant that he moves around at a snail's pace. How could he have made it up to that cliff where the burn started? No, the culprit has to be a young person."

"That's logical reasoning. And I think Saul is sweet on Frankie Cantrell—did you see the way he looked after her when she came by the barn? It's nice to see her back on the Chaparral again, even if it took the fire to bring her home. But several men other than Saul had pumped fuel that day and Guy wasn't one of them." Strapping on her safety belt, she settled back in the seat. "Besides, what would be Guy's motive?"

"Rosa, if we knew the motive, our search would probably be over."

"That's true enough," she agreed.

A half mile later, they reached an intersecting dirt road that ran north and south. North led directly to the Pine Ridge Ranch, and Rosalinda deliberately kept her gaze from drifting in that direction. It wasn't that she was trying to keep her relationship with Tyler a secret, but the less her nosey partner knew, the better.

As for seeing Tyler, she'd not had another chance to be with him since that night they'd returned from the cabin. In the past few days the two of them had spoken on the phone twice, their last conversation taking place three days ago. During that call, he'd informed Rosalinda that he and Santo were going to be out of town for a couple of days on a horse-buying trip, but he wanted to see her as soon as they could get together again.

Realizing it was taking Hank an inordinate amount of time to pull onto the crossroad, she looked over at him. "What are you waiting for? The light to change?"

He grinned at her sarcasm. "I was just about to ask you if you wanted me to turn left. You might want to go up to the Pine Ridge Ranch and say hi to the owner before we leave the area."

It was true she was aching to see Tyler again. Since the two of them had made love, he'd consumed her thoughts. Being connected to him physically had been incredible. It had drawn her to him in ways she'd never felt before. But sharing her past with him had somehow been even more intimate. Now her thoughts alternated between euphoria and downright fear. Had she found the man of her dreams, or had she climbed back into a dangerous pit? She couldn't answer that. She only knew that she wanted to feel his arms around her. She wanted to hear him say he needed her and wanted to be with her just as much as she wanted to be with him. But so far he'd not said anything that would lead her to believe he was thinking in future terms or that he wanted to take their relationship to a deeper level.

It's too soon for that, Rosa. Besides, he made it pretty clear that you shouldn't expect any promises from him any time soon.

Trying to ignore the voice in her head, she scowled at Hank. "Who told you that you should try to be a comedian?"

He snorted with amusement. "You don't have to tell me you're hung up on the rancher. I know you are."

Had she really changed that much since she'd met Tyler? If Hank could see a difference in her, then what was Tyler seeing? "Oh. How did you figure that out?"

Hank answered, "That dreamy look that comes in your eyes for no reason."

"Hmm. For all you know I might be dreaming about a bowl of ice cream."

He grunted. "Ice cream doesn't produce the smoke I'm seeing in those brown eyes of yours."

She pointed to the right-hand junction of the road. "Let's get going, genius. We need to talk to Brady about the discrepancies we found in our interviews today. And if we don't get back to headquarters soon, he'll be heading home."

"All right, all right. I guess that means no stopping for pie at the Blue Mesa," he said doggedly.

"It means no stopping for anything."

Later that evening, after they'd discussed their findings with Brady, Rosalinda was in her office typing up the last of her interview notes, when the phone on her desk rang.

Seeing it was the dispatcher, she quickly punched the flashing button and said, "Yes, Bette?"

"There's a call for you on line four, Rosa. It's from a Gib

Easton. Want me to put it through or tell him you're not available?"

Gib? Why on earth would he be calling her at headquarters? Surely not to invite her to supper. He'd use her personal cell for that. Something had to be wrong.

"No. I'll take the call, Bette. Thanks." She ended the connection to the dispatcher, then punched the button for the line where Gib was waiting. "Gib? Are you there?"

"Sure am. Sorry to interrupt you at work, Rosa. I lost the cell number you gave me."

"That's okay, Gib. I'm only dealing with paperwork at the moment."

"Well, something has happened and I didn't want to wait around to tell you about it."

Her heart went from a nervous thud to an all-out gallop. "Has Tyler been hurt?"

"No. Ain't nothing like that. But he could be hurt if you don't persuade him to—well—" He broke off abruptly and then returned in a low, almost whispering voice. "I don't want to go into the whole thing on the phone. But he got a call from his sister today. The news wasn't good. Ty's mother has taken real sick."

Stunned by this turn of events, Rosalinda stared at the wall while her mind spun with questions. "So Ty is back from his horse-buying trip?"

"Yeah. He made it home about an hour ago. He'd hardly gotten in the house when he got the call."

"How did he take the news about his mother?"

"He told me she was sick, maybe dyin'. Then walked out of the house. Haven't seen him since."

Rosalinda pressed a hand to her forehead. She could almost feel the pain that Tyler must be going through. There were still lots of things she had yet to learn about Tyler, but one thing she did know, if there was one person on earth that he loved, it was his mother.

"I go off duty in an hour. I'll come over straight after that," she promised.

Rosalinda hardly remembered making the drive from headquarters in Carrizozo over to the Pine Ridge Ranch. Her mind kept going over what she could possibly say to him. What she needed to say. He might even resent her talking to him about his mother.

By the time she parked in front of the house, dread had settled in the pit of her stomach. Yet at the same time her heart was yearning to see him, to help him in any way she could.

As soon as she knocked on the front door, Gib stepped out to join her on the front porch. "Tyler still hasn't come back to the house. Sawyer said the last time he saw him Ty was down at the paddock where they keep the weanling colts and fillies. Do you know where that is?"

Rosalinda nodded. "I think so. It's the little pasture on past the stables. I'll go look for him there."

She turned to go, but paused as Gib called to her, "Rosa, as soon as he sees you he's going to know I've been meddlin'. But I don't care how mad he gets. For a long time he's needed to face things with his folks. I never thought there was a chance for that to happen until you came along. That's why I called you."

Stunned by the older man's remark, she stared at him. "Are you thinking I can talk him into going to Texas to see his family?"

"If you can't make the man go, then it ain't possible."

Rosalinda's head swung back and forth. "You're putting too much faith in me, Gib. I don't carry that much weight with Ty."

The white-haired cook leveled a shrewd smile at her. "I think you're gonna learn different."

Now wasn't the time to argue that point, Rosalinda decided. "All right. I'll see what I can do."

She hurried off the porch and down the trail to the ranch yard. As she passed by the barns and cattle pens, she saw a herd of steers lined up at rows of feed troughs. Across the way, lights burned in the bunkhouse and the faint sound of voices could be heard within. Apparently, the men had called it quits for the day, except for Tyler.

When she finally reached the weanling paddock, it was already growing dark, but she could see enough to pick up his silhouette among the horses.

At the fence, she paused, watching as he rubbed manes and scratched ears. Even from this distance, she could see the baby horses loved and trusted him. And he drew solace from them.

I get excitement from watching a calf born or a foal running at its mother's side.

Tyler had said those words to her the morning she'd first met him. And now she understood exactly what he'd meant by them. He might have built this ranch to prove a point, but in doing so, he'd made himself a home, she thought. But would she ever be a part of it? If he couldn't allow his own family into his life, how could he ever hope to have one of his own?

This isn't about your dreams now, Rosa. This is all about Tyler and what he needs.

With that reminder rolling through her head, Rosalinda climbed over the tall board fence and walked across the lush grass. The horses quickly shied to one side and stood staring curiously at her as she walked up to Tyler.

"Sorry I frightened them away," she said.

"Don't worry. Give them a few minutes and they'll be all

over you." He turned to face her. "This is a surprise. I wasn't expecting to see you. You're not on duty tonight?"

"No. I'm here because Gib called me. And frankly, I wish you had."

His jaw tight, he looked away from her. "That old codger never could mind his own business."

"You *are* his business, Ty." Stepping forward, she laid a hand on his forearm. "Did you not want me to know about your mother?"

His gaze swung back to her face and this time she could see his green eyes were full of torment. "It's not that, Rosa. The news hit me so hard I can't think. I don't want to think."

Suddenly he latched on to her shoulders and pulled her tight against him. "Oh, Rosa, she's the only person left in my family who really matters to me. If something happens to her it will be like—well, like they're all dead. Do you understand?"

The rawness in his voice caused her throat to burn and with her arms tight around his waist, she clung to him, her cheek pressed to shoulder. "Yes. I think I do. That's why I believe you should go to her. If you want to tell the rest of your family to go to hell, then so be it. But don't let them keep you from being with the person you love. Before it's too late."

For long moments he didn't respond, and then his hands stirred against her shoulders, and she lifted her face up to his. This time when she looked into his eyes, there was a sparkle of light that resembled something like hope.

"You're right, Rosa. I will go. If you'll go with me."

If he'd not been holding on to her, Rosalinda was certain she would have toppled over backward.

"Go with you? Are you serious?"

"I've never been more serious in my life. I won't make the trip back to Austin without you."

She'd be facing the very people who'd hurt him. Possibly

even his ex-wife. How could she handle that? "But, Ty, your family doesn't know me. I'd only be in the way. And you—"

"I need you, Rosa."

The man she was coming to love needed her, and that was all that really mattered. She gave him a wobbly smile. "When do you want to go? I'll have to see if I can juggle my schedule at work."

"I'll try to book a flight for us in the morning," he said.

Since they were smack in the middle of the arson case, Rosalinda had to do some major maneuvering to get two days leave from work. Thankfully, Sheriff Hamilton had understood and encouraged her to take the time she needed.

Now, as Tyler negotiated the rental car through the Austin streets, toward the hospital where Edie Pickens was being treated, Rosalinda's gaze kept straying over to his stern profile. Throughout the short flight from Ruidoso to Austin, he'd not spoken much and she'd understood his thoughts were preoccupied with his mother.

Inside the hospital, they traveled the elevator up to the fifth floor, then searched until they found Edie's room number. Rosalinda half expected him to pause and collect himself before he entered the room. Instead, he simply reached for her hand and opened the door.

Despite the medical equipment in the room, Rosalinda's gaze went to the woman in the bed. She had very dark hair threaded faintly with silver. Her oval face was very pale, except for her cheeks, and they were bright pink and slightly puffy. The faint outline of her body beneath the bedcovers revealed her build was tall and slender. At the moment, her eyes were closed and she appeared to be unaware of their presence.

Rosalinda was wondering whether Tyler would attempt to wake her, when a woman suddenly stepped out of the private bathroom. Guessing her to be somewhere near forty years of age, she had brown hair and green eyes that vaguely resembled Tyler's and she was staring at them with complete shock.

"Ty! My God! I didn't know you were coming."

"I didn't know it myself until late last night," he told her, then gestured toward Rosalinda. "Constance, I'd like you to meet Rosalinda."

The other woman extended her hand out to Rosalinda. "Nice to meet you, Rosalinda."

Constance Pickens appeared very Texan with her bold jewelry, carefully made-up face and clothes that looked like they came straight from Neiman-Marcus. What surprised Rosalinda was the warm twang in her voice and the welcoming grip of her hand. She'd not expected that from Tyler's sister and she could only hope the men of the family would be half as affable.

"Connie? Who is it? Has someone come to visit?"

Tyler's sister turned toward the bed and the weak sound of their mother's voice.

"Yes," she told the woman. "Someone you've not seen in a long time."

Constance motioned for Tyler, and with his hand at Rosalinda's back, the two of them moved deeper into the room. Once they reached the foot of the bed, Rosalinda could see an oxygen tube in the woman's nose and electrode patches attached to her chest. Nearby, a monitor displayed her heartbeat and blood pressure.

Edie's expression was guarded as she squinted up at Tyler. And then suddenly recognition flashed across her face and she gasped sharply.

"Ty!"

"Yes, Mom," he said quietly. "It's Ty."

One of her hands reached weakly up to him and Ty quickly clasped it between the two of his, then bent to place a kiss on her forehead.

Edie's eyes squeezed tightly shut, and Rosalinda could hardly bear to see the tears slipping from the corners of the woman's eyes.

"You shouldn't have come, Ty. Your father..."

As his mother's words trailed away on a weary sigh, a muscle jumped in Tyler's cheek. "I'll deal with Dad. Don't worry about that," he gently assured her. "Don't worry about anything. Just concentrate on getting well."

Her eyes opened, and as she studied him through her tears, her lips trembled. She started to speak, and a spate of coughing struck her. Once it was over, her head fell limply to the pillow as she struggled to regain her breath. "I didn't think you'd ever come back to Texas," she said finally. "I didn't think I'd ever see you again."

He stroked his mother's hair in the same soft manner he'd stroked the weanling's manes. "I haven't heard from you in a long time, Mom. You should've told me that you've been sick."

"I haven't had any problems until lately. Now the doctor says I need a pacemaker. Just imagine. Your mother needs a battery to keep her motor going. I hope they use one with a long cell life," she joked.

"Mother! That's not funny," Constance scolded her.

Edie glared at her daughter. "Why not joke about it? Trent does." She turned her attention back to Tyler, and this time she looked at him with something akin to fear. "Have you seen Trent yet? Or your father?"

"No."

She shook her head just as another round of coughing hit her. Finally, she was able to say, "Warren is going to raise some hell when he finds out you're here."

"Let him raise it. He can't hurt me anymore, Mom. And I'm sure as hell not going to stand by and let him hurt you. I think when you get well it's high time you come out to New Mexico for a very long visit."

Rosalinda glanced over to Constance to see how his sister was taking Tyler's suggestion. The younger woman looked mildly surprised. Probably because she'd not expected her brother to make those sorts of waves with their father. As for Rosalinda, she could only imagine how different her life might have turned out if Dale had been strong and forceful and taken the problem with Monique by the horns.

But then she would have never met Tyler, she thought. And things happened for a reason. Just like the fire that had brought them together. Now she could only wonder what might happen to tear them apart.

"Maybe it is," Edie said with a weary sigh. "I'll think about that."

Tyler's hand suddenly returned to Rosalinda's back and he urged her closer to the railing of the bed.

"Mom, I want you to meet Rosalinda. She's very important to me."

Edie's gaze left her son's face to travel over Rosalinda and a strange mix of curiosity and joy filled her eyes.

"Yes, I can see that she is," she said to Tyler as she smiled at Rosalinda. "It's nice to meet you, Rosalinda. I'm happy that you made the trip with my son."

"Rosalinda is a deputy sheriff," he told his mother. "She works for the county where I live."

"Oh, my," Edie responded. "You must be a very brave young woman."

Rosalinda smiled. "Not really," she said modestly. "I just like trying to help people who have been wronged."

At that moment, Constance came to stand at the end of the bed and Tyler took the cue that Edie had talked enough.

Bending over her, he placed a kiss on her cheek. "You're

getting tired, Mom. We'll come back later and visit more. After you've rested."

She latched on to his hand and gripped it. No doubt she feared these few short minutes would be the only ones she'd have with her misplaced son.

"You promise you'll be back?"

"I promise. Now rest."

Before his mother could make any more protest, Tyler urged Rosalinda away from the bed and out of the room. His sister followed them and once they were out in the wide corridor, he turned to her for information.

"What are the doctors saying about her condition? How did this happen anyway? Mother is only sixty years old! She's still young! She should be going strong."

Constance grimaced. "You're right about that. But the stress she's lived under has made her more like a hundred-year-old woman. Some part of her heart is wearing out. The doctors are hoping the pacemaker will deal with it for a while. Later on they expect she'll have to have open-heart surgery."

"I see. And what about her condition right now? The pneumonia?"

"They're pulling the excess fluid from her body and her lungs are reacting positively to the antibiotics. Believe me, Tyler, she's a hundred times better today than last night when I called you."

He released a heavy breath. "I'm grateful that you did."

His sister peered skeptically at him. "Really? I wasn't sure. It's not like we've kept in touch, Ty. I didn't know if you would want to hear from me."

Shrugging, he said, "I never had any quarrel with you, Connie."

"No. But I—" She shook her head in a self-deprecating way. "I've always felt badly because I never stepped up and took your side in things. You know how Dad is. It's easier just to stay out of his way. As for Trent, he behaved horribly. And DeeDee, my God, Ty, you made a great escape there. Actually, those two deserve each other. Trent is getting—well, I'll let you see things for yourself. You are going out to the ranch, aren't you?"

He glanced at Rosalinda. "Yes. For a while. But Rosalinda and I will be staying the night here in Austin."

"Then hopefully I'll see you again before you leave." Stepping forward, she gave him a tight hug. "I'm so glad you're here."

"Thanks, Connie. Tell Mom I'll see her later."

After assuring Tyler she'd give their mother the message, Constance waved them off, and they walked down the corridor to the nearest elevator.

As they stepped into the cage, Rosalinda looked over at his strained profile. "Your mother is going to get better, Ty. I feel certain of that."

"She looked awful." He jabbed the button that would lower them to the ground floor. "She used to be a beautiful woman, Rosa. But living with Dad for forty years has taken a toll on her."

"Why has she stayed? Because she loves him or fears him?"

He grimaced. "A little of both, I think."

Rosalinda suddenly thought about Daisy Martell and how she'd advised the young woman to make changes in her life. Edie Pickens was much older than Daisy, but it was never too late to reach for happiness.

"When you mentioned visiting New Mexico to her, I could see a light suddenly spark in her eyes. It would be good for her to be with you. She's already missed so many years with you."

"After she gets out of the hospital and back on her feet, I'm going to make sure she spends time on my ranch. And I'm going to make that clear to Dad."

The elevator opened and they stepped past a group of people waiting to enter. As they headed toward the huge glass doors that would take them to the parking area, she asked, "Are we going out to the Rocking P now?"

"We are. Why? Are you worried?"

"I'd be lying if I said I wasn't. As a law officer, I've seen—well, family fights can get out of hand."

"There won't be any fighting, Rosa."

"Arguments lead to explosions," she reasoned.

"There won't be any of that, either."

By now they were out on the sidewalk and they paused in the shade of a crepe myrtle tree. A hot, humid wind was whipping her hair in all directions and as she lifted her hands to hold it down, he slipped his arms around her waist and pulled her close.

"Look, Rosa, my main purpose for coming here is Mom. As for my father and brother, I can't change who they are. I wouldn't want to try. But I figure they think I stayed away all these years because I'm not man enough to face them. They need to know different. And this is something I should have done a long time ago."

Releasing the hold on her flying hair, she placed her hand against his cheek and somehow the feel of his day-old whiskers comforted her, reminded her that he was his own man and walked his own path.

"And what about DeeDee?"

"What about her?"

"You might see her, too."

With a wry shake of his head, he said, "DeeDee can't hurt me anymore. Now let's get going."

On the way to the car, Tyler's words continued to echo in her ears.

DeeDee can't hurt me anymore. Dale had said those very

same words about Monique and look how that had turned out, she thought, sickly. The woman had very nearly killed her.

But DeeDee wasn't a psycho. And Rosalinda was now an officer of the law. She was trained and capable to deal with violent people, she reminded herself. However, she wasn't trained to protect her heart. And now, more than ever, she was beginning to see that coming here with Tyler was exposing it to all sorts of dangers. Because slowly and surely she could feel herself falling in love with him and the realization left her more vulnerable than she'd ever felt in her life.

Chapter Twelve

The Rocking P Ranch was on a vast stretch of land situated northwest of Austin. As they drove through the green rolling hills dotted with live oaks and mesquite trees, Rosalinda could only think how different the area was from Tyler's ranch. This land was gentle, the lush meadows undulating into another. Tyler's land was rough and tough and breathtaking. So very much like him, she thought.

"We're almost to the house," he said, his voice cutting into her thoughts. "I'm sure you're tired. We've been traveling most of the morning. And meeting Mom under those circumstances couldn't have been easy for you."

Outside the window, a white board fence bordered the dirt road and stretched as far as the eye could see. Massive live oaks shaded sections of the road and dotted the pastures. Beneath their draped limbs, black cattle sought relief from the burning sun, while at others, horses dozed and swished their tails at the pestering flies.

"Don't worry about me," she assured him. "I just want everything to turn out okay for you."

Reaching across the small console, he clutched her hand. "Everything will turn out okay, Rosa. As long as you're with me."

What did he mean exactly? Was he trying to say he loved and needed her? She would have liked to ask him. But now was not the time go into it.

Up ahead a tall scalloped wall built of yellow sandstone came into view. And in the center of the rock fence, an iron gate embellished with the ranch's brand stood imposingly.

Once they reached it, Tyler pressed a button and the gates mechanically opened to allow them entrance. As the Rocking P ranch house came into full view, Rosalinda leaned slightly forward and stared at the majestic sight.

The massive two-story structure was built in Spanish style with beige textured walls and terracotta shingles. The windows and doors were trimmed with dark brown wood while a ground-level porch ran the full width of the front.

Live oaks and cottonwoods created a deep shade upon the manicured lawn, while blooming crepe myrtles and climbing bougainvilleas splashed the area with colors of white, red and magenta. How could such a splintered family live in such splendid beauty? she wondered.

"This is where your parents live?" she asked, trying not to appear awestruck.

"Yes. This is where I grew up. My paternal grandparents first started the ranch, but they both passed on many years ago." He gestured toward the north. "The house I built for DeeDee is about a mile over in that direction."

"You built a house just for her?"

He grimaced. "She said she wanted more privacy. And I was trying to make her happy. I didn't know then that I was attempting an impossible feat."

He must have been crazy about the woman to have gone to such lengths to please her, Rosalinda thought. But it could be that he tried so hard with DeeDee simply because he'd not wanted to admit failure. The same way she'd fought so uselessly to hang on to Dale. Funny how her relationship with Tyler had opened her eyes to the mistakes she'd made back then. Not only that, he was making her view the future in an entirely different light. Instead of focusing solely on being a good deputy, she was daring to dream about having a family.

A circular drive took them directly in front of the house. As she and Tyler walked up to the door, she told herself not to be intimidated by the wealth around her or the idea of meeting Warren Pickens. He might bully his wife, but Rosalinda wouldn't allow him to strike fear in her. These past few years on her own had taught her to stand up for herself and her beliefs.

Tyler was pushing the doorbell when the sound of a vehicle skidding on gravel had them both looking over their shoulders to see a red pickup truck had braked to a jarring halt behind their rental car.

A tall man in cowboy gear, complete with a straw hat and spurs, climbed down from the cab and strode toward them. Almost instantly, Rosalinda decided he had to be Tyler's twin. Although they didn't resemble each other in facial features or coloring, there was something about this man's lithe stride and the carriage of his head that reminded her of Tyler.

"The maid has bad knees. It takes her forever to answer the ring," he said as he approached them. "Can I help—?"

His words abruptly trailed away as he stepped onto the porch and stared straight at Tyler.

"Hello, Trent."

The other man's mouth fell open and his tanned complexion turned the color of a mushroom. For a split second, Rosalinda thought he was going to keel over in a faint.

"Ty! What are you doing here?" he finally got out.

Tyler's bland expression didn't change. "I flew in to see Mom."

Trent pulled off the straw and swatted it against the side of his leg. The removal of the hat revealed a shock of tawny-colored hair clipped close to his head. He ran his fingers through the flattened strands while seeming to attempt to collect himself.

"Oh. So you got the news that she was sick."

"Connie called me."

The corners of his mouth turned downward. "She would. When Mom was out of it with high fever she kept calling your name. Guess Connie thought it would do her some good to see you."

No hugs or smiles, Rosalinda thought sadly. Not even a handshake. But how did a man greet the one who'd stolen his wife from him? Civility would be the most to expect, she supposed.

"She's in bad shape," Tyler said.

Trent made a dismissive wave of his hand as though his brother were discussing a cow or horse. "Mom is a tough old boot. She'll be fine." Walking past Rosalinda without any sort of acknowledgment of her presence, he went over to the door and opened it. "Y'all might as well come in and make yourselves comfortable."

They followed him into the house and passed through a long foyer before finally entering a large, richly furnished, sitting room.

"Is Dad home?" Tyler asked. "I didn't see him at the hospital. Hasn't he been staying near Mom?"

Trent chuckled and Rosalinda couldn't decide whether the sound was an expression of amusement or sarcasm. As far as she was concerned, neither was appropriate. And just in these few short minutes since Tyler's twin had arrived, she was beginning to see exactly how different these two men were.

"You know Dad, he hates hospitals," Trent said. "Reminds him of his own mortality, I guess. And God knows the man never intends to die." His spurs jangled as he crossed the carpeted floor. At a wet bar he picked up a bottle of Kentucky bourbon and splashed a goodly amount into a squat tumbler. "You two want a drink? I've had a hell of a mornin'. I need one."

Because he'd found his long-lost brother on the porch? As she watched the man toss back the whiskey, she realized it was Trent who was shaken by the sight of Tyler. Not the other way around.

"No, thank you," Rosalinda told him.

Moving to Rosalinda's side, Tyler curved his arm against the back of her waist. Trent set his glass aside and walked over to where they stood.

"I'm Trent Pickens," he introduced himself to Rosalinda. "Tyler's twin. I'm sure he's told you about me."

From the corner of her eye, she glanced at Tyler. His jaw was tight, but other than that she couldn't read what he was possibly thinking at this moment.

"I'm Rosalinda Lightfoot. And yes, Tyler's mentioned you."

He didn't bother to shake her hand; instead, he threw back his head and laughed. "Mentioned?" He darted a cocky glance at Tyler. "Man, I thought after all we've been through together I'd deserve more than a mention."

"Rosa and I have better things to discuss," Tyler said.

"Oooh—ouch. I guess I had that coming."

Rosalinda was wondering if Trent Pickens was a complete idiot, or if he'd been nipping at the bourbon bottle more than once this morning, when an elderly woman with a gray pixie cut and an extremely thin frame walked into the room. Since an apron was tied over her dark skirt and white blouse, she figured this had to be the maid with bad knees.

"Verbena!" Tyler hurried over to the woman and gave her a hug that lifted her slight form completely off the floor.

"Mr. Tyler! You put me down before you break my old bones!" she ordered with a laugh. As soon as he set the woman on the floor, the maid stepped away in order to eye him fully. "Oh! Oh, my! What a sight for sore eyes. You look good. Real good. I was so happy when Miss Connie called you."

Tyler grinned at the woman who'd once fed him cookies and dried his tears. "And you still look as pretty as a June mornin'. How have you been?"

"Pining to see your face again." Beaming with pleasure, she latched on to his arm. "Now you and your beautiful young lady get freshened up and join me back in the kitchen. When Miss Connie told me you'd be coming, I started cooking, so I've got all sorts of good things for you to eat."

"We'll be there in a few minutes," he promised.

Verbena left the room, and Trent rubbed his hands together in a gesture of nervous anticipation. Was he already thinking there was going to be trouble between their father and Tyler?

"So how long are you going to stay around, brother?"

"Long enough to see Dad and then leave."

Trent's brows lifted with surprise. "You're not going to show Rosalinda around the ranch?" Then before Tyler could make any sort of reply, he went on in a sarcastic voice, "DeeDee will be hurt if she misses seeing you."

"I'll just bet," Tyler muttered. Then with his hand on Rosalinda's arm, he guided her out of the room and away from his twin brother.

Down a short hallway, he pointed to a door. "There's the powder room. Take all the time you need. When you're finished just follow this hallway to the end and you'll find the kitchen. I'll wait for you there."

She caught him by the arm. "Before you go, Ty, I—" She paused and shook her head. "This is probably the wrong time for me to say anything, but your brother is either the most insensitive man I've ever met or he's got mental issues."

He glanced over his shoulder as though he half expected to see Trent following them. "Sorry, Rosa. I realize this has to be uncomfortable for you. But I wanted you with me. To see Mom. And to be honest, a part of me wanted my family to see the woman in my life. But I should have stopped to think what I might be subjecting you to."

Not caring who might see them, she slipped her arms around his neck and hugged him close. "Oh, Ty, don't worry about me. With my job I hear things I wouldn't repeat to anyone in a dark closet. It's just that to hear your brother's remarks and see his attitude toward you—well, angry doesn't quite describe how it makes me feel."

Down the hallway toward the front of the house, the sound of a door opening, then slamming shut, reverberated back to them. Seconds later, an engine fired to life, then quickly faded away.

"Guess that was all he wanted to see of me," Tyler spoke the obvious.

"I think I'd be relieved."

He nodded glumly. "Trent could always be obnoxious, but the years have clearly changed him. Big-time. I figure that was probably the second or third drink he's had this morning."

"That crossed my mind, too." She kissed his cheek, then eased out of his arms. "Go on to the kitchen and relax, Ty. I'll be there in just a few minutes," she promised.

When Tyler reached the kitchen, Verbena had already set two places at a red chrome-and-Formica table and chairs.

Instead of taking a seat, he walked over to where the older woman was at the sink, filling two glasses with tap water.

"Verbena, you don't have to go to all this trouble. Rosa and I can wait on ourselves."

Frowning at him, she carried the drinks over to the table. "It's lunchtime and I know you've not had time to eat yet. This is my job, Ty. God only knows why I keep doing it. I've tried to quit, but Edie always begs me not to go."

Lifting his hat from his head, he walked over and hung it on a wall peg. "I'm sure she does. You're the only one around here she can truly depend on and trust."

With a hand on her hip, she turned to face him. "And how would you know that? You haven't been here in what? Nine, ten years?"

"Almost ten," he answered. "But Mom has called and sent letters. She tells me things."

"Humph. Probably only skims the surface of what goes on around here. It's like a regular soap opera, Ty. Sometimes I tell myself I can't quit just because I want to see what happens in the next episode."

"You've been with the family since I was a little boy. You've seen a lot of things happen around here." He moved across the room to where she stood by the table. "When did Trent become such a mess? We'd hardly walked into the house a few minutes ago, when he started belting back bourbon like a villain in the Long Branch Saloon."

Verbena shook her head. "Trent's always been a mess. You know that. After you left, he got worse. And now that him and DeeDee have split the sheets, he's sliding straight toward the hog wallow."

Tyler was stunned by this news, although he didn't know why he should be surprised. Both his ex-wife and his brother were self-centered and irresponsible. That sort of pairing could do nothing but implode. “DeeDee and Trent have divorced?”

“Not yet. But Trent stays over here most of the time. He’s trying to figure out how to protect his holdings without DeeDee taking him to the cleaners.” With a disapproving sniff, she walked back over to the cabinet. “If you ask me, he deserves to be taken to the cleaners. Serve him right for what he did to you.”

“Ending up with DeeDee as his wife is quite a punishment in itself, Verbena.”

His statement brought the woman’s head around and she studied Tyler with amazement. “Is that all you have to say about the man? I figured you’d want to see his head on a chopping block.”

Tyler gazed over toward the windows, but beyond the paned glass he was seeing the past, not the shaded yard. “Maybe a long time ago I would have liked that.” And maybe even a month ago he would have liked to knock Trent on his can, he thought dourly. But meeting Rosalinda and seeing her courage and strength had done something to all that anger he’d been carrying around. Now it seemed like a senseless waste of time and energy. “Back when I was trying so hard to please Dad,” he went on. “But not now. It doesn’t give me any pleasure to see Trent unhappy.”

“Hmm. You not only look different, Ty. You’ve changed on the inside. And it all looks mighty fine to me,” Verbena said proudly.

At that moment Rosalinda stepped into the room. Tyler walked over to meet her and reveled in the pleasure of curling his arm around her slender waist. “Come over here and let me introduce you properly to Verbena. She’s a fixture here on the ranch.”

Verbena winked at Rosalinda. “That’s right. When I’m not cooking or cleaning, I stand in for a pole lamp or a coatrack.”

Smiling warmly, Rosalinda said, "I'm very glad to meet you, Verbena. Call me Rosa."

Instead of shaking Rosalinda's hand, the other woman grabbed her up in a hug. "Rosa, you must be mighty special for Tyler to bring you here to the Rocking P."

As Tyler watched, a blush spread across Rosalinda's face, he realized just how much their relationship had grown since they'd first met. And bringing her here to meet his family, even as dysfunctional as they were, still meant something to him. It meant he was crazy in love with the woman. But did it mean he wanted to try marriage once again? That was a question he was going to have to answer soon. For his own sake and for Rosalinda's.

"Well, we've not known each other all that long," Rosa told her. "But I think he's beginning to like me."

"I have a feeling he does," Verbena replied with a knowing chuckle, then made a shooing motion toward the table. "You two go sit. I'll bring the food over. I made enchiladas, since they were always your favorite."

After they were seated and Verbena had laid the food out in front of them, she took a seat at the opposite end of the table and sipped from a tall glass of sweet tea.

Between bites, Tyler said, "Dad wasn't at the hospital with Mom. Where is he?"

"Oh, him and John Robert went to the cattle auction over in Llano. I expect they'll be back before dark."

"So John Robert is still the foreman around here?"

"Yeah. Guess he's like me, he'll be around the place 'til he dies." Glancing at him over the edge of her glass, she asked, "What about Gib? Is he still with you?"

"Yes. And I guess he'll be with me until he dies," Tyler told her.

Verbena smiled, and Tyler thought he saw a mist of tears in the old woman's eyes. "I'm glad to hear it. I miss him. But he was smart to go with you. He doesn't have to see the Pickens family trying to claw each other apart."

Tyler had felt those claws, too. And at one time they'd cut him deep. Strange how he felt immune to them now. "Has Dad gone to see Mom since she entered the hospital?" Tyler asked.

"He was with her when she was admitted. After that, he hasn't been back. Says he'll see her when they get her fixed and she comes home."

Tyler shared a disgusted look with Rosalinda. "Trent has changed, but I guess Dad hasn't."

"Guess you'll find that out when he gets home."

"Yeah. I guess I will."

After they finished eating, Tyler showed Rosalinda around the house. He'd not felt particularly inclined to visit his old room, but when she asked to see it, he couldn't disappoint her.

As they walked across the upstairs landing, she said, "I had to share my bedroom with my sister. But this house is so huge I suppose you and Trent had your own separate rooms."

"When Dad had the house built, I think he was planning on lots of kids, but after Mom had us twins, something happened and she couldn't get pregnant anymore. Just as well, I suppose. She had her hands full with us."

When they reached the door to his old bedroom, he paused with his hand on the knob. "No telling what's in here now. After we were married, DeeDee and I didn't use this room. She wanted one of the larger bedrooms. So this one is probably just used for a storage room now."

"No matter," she said with a gentle smile. "I can still imagine what it looked like when you were a little boy."

Tyler opened the door, then followed behind her as she stepped into the room. But after two or three steps, he came to an abrupt halt and stared around him in wonder.

"I can't believe this!"

His muttered exclamation had Rosalind looking back at him. "What's wrong?"

"This room. It's exactly like I left it years ago."

"Are you serious?"

He strode over to the four-poster bed and touched a hand to the brown spread. "This is the same bedcover." Turning on his boot heel, he made a complete sweep of the room. "The curtains are the same. And my trophies and ribbons that I won at the livestock shows are there on the shelves. The photos and mementoes I collected are there, too."

Dazed, he walked over to the pine desk where he used to do his homework. A plastic model of the great race horse Dash For Cash still sat on one corner. He picked up the model and stared at it while his mind whirled with questions, doubts and even hopes.

"I can't imagine what this means, Rosa. The last words Dad said to me were to get the hell out and don't come back." He placed the horse back on the desk, then rubbed a hand over his weary eyes. "I figured he'd probably had Mom get rid of all this stuff that I'd left behind."

"Maybe he did, but she refused," Rosa suggested.

"No. No way would she ever defy him. There's some other reason for this."

Walking over to him, Rosalinda laid a hand on his arm. "Why did your dad say those things to you?"

He shrugged. "Dear God, Rosa, now when I try to remember all about that time it's like a foggy dream. None of it makes sense. I only know that back then I was full up to here with him telling me what to do, how to act, how to deal with my wife and Trent." He used a hand to mark a spot just below his chin. "I'd had enough of his ramrod ways and I told him I was leaving. I didn't want to be a part of the Rocking P anymore."

"So he didn't try to talk you out of it? Try to stop you from leaving?"

Tyler shook his head. "He understood it would have been useless. So he didn't try. Instead, he told me to never come back."

"But here you are," she said softly.

He let out a heavy breath. "Yeah. Here I am. Even if it is only for a day."

Rosalinda moved away from him and wandered over to the windows that overlooked the back of the house and the working ranch yard in the far distance. As she gazed at the view, she said, "Maybe it hurt him too much to say anything else."

Walking up behind her, he slipped his arms around her waist and linked his fingers over her stomach. "I'd like to believe that, Rosa. But Warren Pickens doesn't feel any pain."

He'd barely gotten the words out when a red pickup truck, much like the one Trent had been driving, rolled to a stop at the backyard fence and two men climbed out of the cab. The driver took off walking in the direction of the ranch yard. The other one headed to the house and even from this distance Tyler could see it was his father.

Everything inside him tightened with dread. "There he is now, Rosa. Do you want to go down with me to see him? Or stay up here?"

She turned and gave him a brief, reassuring smile. "I think it would be best if you first talked with him alone. I'll come down later."

"All right." He kissed her lightly on the lips, then left the room before he could convince himself that Warren Pickens didn't warrant a word from his estranged son.

By the time Tyler reached the downstairs landing, he could hear his father yelling from somewhere in the vicinity of the kitchen.

"Verbena! Where the hell are you? I want some fresh coffee! And that doesn't mean I want it two hours from now!"

"You want it on a silver platter?" the old woman bravely called back to him.

Warren's answer was the slam of a door. Tyler continued through the house while guessing the sound had come from his father's office, where he did his own bookkeeping for the Rocking P Ranch.

When Tyler arrived at the closed door, he'd expected to feel stiff with nerves and full of dread. Instead, he felt strangely calm and he wondered what sort of cataclysmic event had taken place inside him. Seeing his mother so ill? Realizing he was ready to love again? He didn't know. But he welcomed the steady strength flowing through him.

Rapping a short knock on the door, he stepped into the dimly lit room. With his back to him, Warren continued to dig through a drawer in a file cabinet.

"That was fast enough. You still have any of that pie left? The chocolate one."

"I'm not Verbena," Tyler said.

Warren Pickens whirled around to stare at him and for a moment Tyler thought his father was the one who was going to die of heart failure instead of his mother. Warren had aged considerably since Tyler had last laid eyes on him. His leathery skin was creased with wrinkles and the corners of his mouth drooped with the shape of his walrus mustache. Blue eyes that were once vibrant and full of life were now faded and dull.

"Tyler! How— Nobody told me you were coming!"

"Nobody knew it."

He wiped a hand over his face as though he didn't trust what he was seeing. Then, using his back to push the drawer closed, he walked over to the large desk and sank into a big leather chair.

"What are you doing here?" he finally asked.

"I came to see Mom. Connie phoned me. Do you understand how seriously ill she is?"

He glowered at Tyler. "You think I'm stupid?"

"No. I think you're an indifferent, unfeeling bastard."

"Is that what you came here to tell me?"

"I'd not planned it. But you asked." Tyler moved across the room and eased into a straight-backed chair that was positioned in front of Warren's desk. "I mainly came to tell you that when Mom gets better I'm taking her out to the Pine Ridge Ranch to live with me for a while."

Warren's eyes narrowed. "And what is this Pine Ridge Ranch?" he asked sardonically. "Ten acres with a cow/calf pair on it?"

Ignoring his father's hateful sarcasm, he said, "I'll let Mom tell you about it."

Warren's pale face suddenly grew red with anger. "Edie isn't going to tell me about anything of yours because she's not going to New Mexico. She's coming right back here!"

Tyler merely smiled. "Sorry, but you're finished running roughshod over her, Dad. You can turn Trent into an alcoholic and ruin the rest of his life, but you're not going to ruin what years Mom has left."

The older man's jaw dropped. "I didn't turn Trent into an alcoholic! DeeDee has done that!"

"And who put him on to her in the first place?"

He spluttered. "I was only trying to save you, Tyler! Hell, I knew she was all wrong for you. And I knew she had eyes for Trent. It was easy to sic him on that airheaded blonde. Those two mealymouths deserve each other."

Tyler's head shook ruefully back and forth. "Did you ever love either of your sons, Dad? Ever since we were little boys, you pitted us against each other. Why?"

Suddenly Warren's shoulders slumped and his face returned to a sickly white. "Keeping a ranch of this size going takes guts and strength, Ty. I realized that someday I'd be too old and one of you would have to take over. I had to see which of you boys could stand up to the task. And the only way I could find out was to test you."

Tyler suddenly felt sick. All the loss and waste. The anger and bitterness. All for nothing. "So who won, Dad? I sure as hell don't see any winners around here."

"You won, boy. By the time you were ten years old I could see you had the guts and the makings to be a rancher. But then you married DeeDee and I didn't want you ruined by the likes of her."

"So you ruined my marriage and my relationship with my brother instead. And I suppose you think I should be grateful to you for that." Rising to his feet, he looked down at his father. "You know, you were right about one thing, I was the one with the guts. Enough of them to walk away from you. And I thank God for that."

He walked out of the study and quietly shut the door behind him.

Chapter Thirteen

On the drive back to Austin, Tyler only made small talk, and Rosalinda understood he wasn't ready to get into his conversation with his father. But it was clear to her that the meeting hadn't gone that well.

Once he'd come back upstairs and collected her from his bedroom, they'd said goodbye to Verbena, then quickly left the ranch. He'd not asked Rosalinda if she wanted to meet Warren Pickens and, frankly, after being exposed to Trent for those few short minutes, she'd been relieved she was being spared the father. If Warren was anything like Tyler's brother, then she didn't want to meet the man.

It was no wonder he'd chosen to live such a quiet, lonely life these past nine years, she thought. The Pickens family had undoubtedly turned him against the whole human race.

Now as they stepped into the plush suite Tyler had reserved for them, the air was blissfully cool from the Texas heat and as Rosalinda sank onto a brocade couch, she realized just how drained the day of traveling and meeting his family had left her.

As she kicked off her heels and massaged her feet, Tyler put their two small bags in the closet, then removed his hat and raked both hands through his hair.

"I don't know about you, Rosa, but I don't want to leave this room tonight."

"You don't plan on visiting your mother again tonight?"

"Connie texted that Mom was too exhausted for another visit tonight. I thought we'd go to the hospital in the morning. Before we have to catch our flight."

"I am tired," she admitted. "Are you?"

He walked over to the couch and sank down close to her side. "I feel like someone threw me in front a truck and it's been rolling over me all afternoon."

He dropped his head against the back of the couch and let out a weary sigh. She reached over and placed her hand over his.

"I wish there was some way I could make it all better for you, Ty. I really do."

He closed his eyes. "I expected things to go bad with Dad. And they did. But during the drive back here to the city, I kept thinking about the things he said to me. Most of them were damned hard to believe. I never imagined he felt that way about me."

She leaned earnestly toward him. "How do you mean?"

Raising his head, he looked at her with a mixture of anguish and wonder. "In his own twisted way, I think he loves me."

Rosalinda gasped. "Oh, Ty! That's good, isn't it? I mean, I got the impression that you thought he hated you."

"I couldn't think anything else. From the time I was a small boy, he goaded and pushed, then exploded when I didn't follow his commands to the letter. He always kept a tight,

tight rein over me while he allowed Trent to go on his merry way. Trent had always appeared to be the apple of his eye while I was the whipping post. All those years he never told me that I was the one he considered the good, responsible son, the only son he had worthy of running and inheriting the Rocking P. Today he decided to let me in on his feelings."

Stunned, Rosalinda's gaze swept his face. "Oh, Ty, to find that out now. Your family's ranch is worth a fortune. Are you now regretting you left? That the ranch won't go to you?"

A wan smile moved his features and the soft gaze he settled on her face made her feel like she was the most special thing in the world to him.

"Owning that ranch was never my dream, Rosa. Now I feel sorry for Trent. Dad set him out for everyone to fawn over and left him there to spoil." He reached for her and pulled her into his arms. "Oh, Rosa, my ranch back home—I never realized how much I loved it until now. And you—I'm so blessed to have you. You're what makes me happy."

The warm, hard strength of his body, the intoxicating scent of his skin and hair muddled the questions and doubts that were racing through her mind. There would be time to try to unravel them all later, she promised herself.

Bringing her face around to his, she spoke against his lips, "You make me very happy, too, Ty. Do you think it's too early for us to go to bed?"

He groaned with pleasure. "I think it's a perfect time," he said. Then, scooping her up in his arms, he carried her to the king-size bed.

Much, much later, after the sky had darkened and the lights of the city twinkled through the plate-glass window, Rosalinda rested her head against Tyler's shoulder and laid her hand upon the steady beat of his heart.

"Here in this room it seems like we're a world away from

everything," she murmured. "Your family. The fire. And tomorrow."

He shifted so that they were facing each other. "I can put all of that out of my mind for a while. But not you, Rosa." He touched the dark tendrils of hair lying against her shoulder, using his forefinger to trace the lush curve of her lower lip. "Today when we were at the ranch I realized that nothing in my life would be the same without you, Rosa. I love you."

Rosalinda's heart had been longing to hear those words, and for the past few weeks, she'd let herself imagine him saying them to her. She'd thought she would feel elated and complete. But so much had happened in the past twenty-four hours that her emotions were on a roller coaster. Hearing his declaration of love felt almost surreal. A part of her wanted to laugh with sheer joy, while at the same time she was close to breaking into tears.

"You don't have anything to say?"

She focused on the rugged line of his lips while she tried to make sense of the feelings that were sweeping her onto the crest of a wave. The ride was exhilarating and frightening at the same time.

"I'm trying to catch my breath," she finally admitted.

A gentle smile touched his face. "Surely I didn't surprise you. I think you've always understood me better than I have myself."

She rubbed the back of her fingers against his cheek. "To be honest, Ty, I think I've been dreaming about you saying those words to me ever since that night outside the Blue Mesa when you kissed me. Even then I felt so drawn to you. But I wasn't expecting to hear this from you tonight."

"I hope that's a roundabout way of saying you love me, too."

A tide of feelings suddenly flooded her, making her voice

low and husky when she spoke. "I do love you, Ty. Very much."

Groaning with relief, he wrapped his arm over her and hugged her tightly to him. "Rosa, ever since that night—ever since that kiss at the Blue Mesa—you've changed my world. Day by day I started to see that hanging on to the past was only ruining my future. A future with you. I want us to be married, soon. If you're one of those women that wants a fancy wedding, then I'll give you time to make the arrangements. But as far as I'm concerned, I'd like to marry you tonight—tomorrow—as soon as possible."

With her hands against his bare shoulders, she levered herself back enough to look at him. "Ty, I've just now learned that you love me. Marriage is an important step. I— We both need time to think about this."

He went very still and she knew her resistance had taken him by surprise. And why not? She'd just made long, passionate love to him. Hadn't she been telling him with every kiss, every touch that she wanted to be with him for the rest of her life?

You do want to be with him forever, Rosa. What the hell is the matter with you anyway? The man of your dreams proposes and you start running backward. You're crazy.

No. She wasn't crazy. She was scared. The moment she'd agreed to marry Dale was when all their troubles had started. From that point on, their relationship and plans for the future had slowly but surely broken into pieces. Senseless as it seemed, she was afraid if she said yes to Tyler's proposal the same thing would happen to them.

"You think I'm not serious?"

His question interrupted her troubled thoughts. "Yes, I believe you're serious. But I think you— Well, so much has happened in the past few days. Especially with your family.

I imagine you need to sort it all out. You need to give me time to sort it all out."

Clearly frustrated, he suddenly scrambled upright and swung his legs over the side of the bed. "Time? Hells bells, Rosa. I've had ten years to think about what my family did to me. I've come to terms with it. What else is there to sort out?"

His words suddenly forced her thoughts in a different direction. Maybe she was the one who needed to come to terms with everything. These past few weeks with Tyler had shown her just how much she'd been missing in her life. And because of him, she'd found the courage to reach for love again. And somewhere along the way, a part of her had begun to dream about marriage and a family. But the moment he'd actually spoken the word to her, something inside her had frozen with fear. How could she explain such irrational feelings and expect him to understand?

Rising up in the bed, she touched a hand to his back. "You just figured out that your dad loves you. That has to change things in your mind. Maybe even your plans for the future."

Amazed by her reasoning, he shook his head. "You weren't listening, Rosa. I said he loves me in a warped way. Not the way a father should really love his son. And even if he did, I wouldn't go back to the Rocking P. My home is in the Capitan Mountains. With you."

"I want to believe that. But seeing your family home today has started me wondering. Your father might be an unforgiving man, but I have the feeling he'd welcome you home in a heartbeat. Probably even deed the Rocking P over to you. And Verbena said that Trent and DeeDee are getting a divorce."

He twisted around to look at with stunned fascination. "What does that have to do with anything?"

She climbed off the bed and reached for the silk robe she'd draped over the back of an armchair. As she wrapped it over her nakedness, she said, "You didn't go see her."

He made a sound of disbelief. "Why would I want to?"

"She obviously doesn't want Trent now. Maybe she realizes she should've never given you up. And maybe you were afraid that seeing her would make you realize you still care for her."

Rising from the bed, he jerked on a pair of white boxer shorts. "Oh, my God, Rosa! Maybe Dale still has the hots for you. Maybe you should make a trip up to Gallop just to make sure all of that is over between you two!"

He was angry now, but then so was she. Angry that he'd shattered her peace of mind. That he was making her sound like a scared little girl. Because, deep down, she was a scared little girl. "You're being crude now."

"And you're being totally unreasonable!" he muttered. Then, with a heavy sigh, he walked up behind her and placed his hands upon her shoulders.

As he drew her back against him, she wanted to turn and bury her face against his chest. She wanted to confess how terrified she was to say the words, *Yes, I'll marry you.*

"I'm sorry," he said softly. "I shouldn't have said that."

Tears burned her eyes. "I shouldn't have said that about DeeDee, either. I know I'm being unreasonable, Ty. But I'm afraid. When I agreed to marry Dale that's when everything fell apart. I don't want that to happen to us. So many things about your family are unsettled."

"Unsettled is putting it mildly, Rosa. They're fractured."

Daring to face him, she turned in his arms and lifted her gaze to his. "You say you're going to bring your mother to live with you on the Pine Ridge Ranch for a while. What do you think will happen if you do?"

"Is that what's bothering you? You don't like the idea of having a meddling mother-in-law around?"

"No! I'm sure I'd grow to love Edie as much as you do. I'm talking about your father. He doesn't sound like a man to simply turn his possessions over without a fight. What if he showed up on your ranch? He could cause all sorts of trouble for you—for us! How would you handle it?"

A look of sudden dawning came over his face. "Okay. I get it now. You're afraid. Afraid that I'll be like Dale. Too weak to handle the situation. Too pathetic to protect the woman I love." Disappointment filled his eyes. "I may not wear a pistol on my hip like you, Rosa. But I'm not a coward. If that's what you think of me, then it's probably best you don't say yes to marrying me now."

She felt sick inside. The more she'd tried to explain herself, the more her doubts had hurt him. "I'm sorry, Ty. The problem isn't you. It's me. I just need time."

"Time for what? Time to decide if I'm man enough for you?" He moved away from her and found his jeans where he'd tossed them on the floor. "Maybe you're the one who should have gone to visit DeeDee. She could've given you all the answers you needed."

She watched him jerk on the jeans and fasten the buttons. "Ty, that isn't fair!"

"Rosa, didn't anyone ever tell you that the only fair in this world is the kind with Ferris wheels and livestock shows?"

She was trying to figure out how she might answer his question when he threw on his shirt and stalked toward the door.

"Where are you going?" she asked.

"Out. And don't bother waiting up for me. I don't know when I'll be back."

"If walking out is your way of handling problems then I'm not so sure we have any kind of future together!" she flung the words at him.

He shut the door behind him and Rosalinda sank into the armchair and waited for the tears in her eyes and the ache in her chest to go away.

* * *

Nearly a week later, Rosalinda had just finished having a cup of coffee with Hank and another deputy and was leaving the Blue Mesa when she heard the light tap of trotting footsteps approach her from behind.

Turning, she was completely surprised to see Daisy Martell. The young woman had missed the self-defense classes last night, and Rosalinda had feared something bad might have happened.

"Deputy Lightfoot, I drove by here in hopes I might see you." Her gaze swept over the badge pinned to Rosalinda's uniform and the weapon strapped to her hip. "Are you working right now?"

"I went off duty a while ago," Rosalinda told her. "Do you need my help? Or if you'd like to talk we can go in the restaurant and have something to drink."

Shaking her head, she said, "I won't keep you that long. I only wanted to let you know that I won't be coming to class anymore. And I wanted to thank you for all that you've done for me."

Rosalinda studied the young woman's heart-shaped face. There was no sign of trauma. In fact, since they'd been standing here on the sidewalk she'd not once glanced around in fear.

"I don't understand, Daisy. I thought you wanted to complete the whole session of classes. Has something happened?"

Daisy suddenly smiled. "I took your advice, Deputy Lightfoot. I reached out for help and someone is here now to take me far away to another state. We'll be leaving tonight. And I wanted to find you and say goodbye. And thanks."

Rosalinda was more than surprised. She would've made bets that Daisy was going to stay in that no-win situation until it self-destructed. The fact that Daisy was getting out and moving on was like spotting a rainbow after a terrible storm.

"I'm so happy for you, Daisy. But I haven't done anything to deserve your thanks. You did it all yourself."

The young woman shook her head. "You don't understand, Deputy Lightfoot. Just seeing a woman like you being so brave and capable inspires a woman like me. And when you talked about finding the courage to make a change, I realized I had to do that. Or I would never be happy or have much of a life at all."

A lump of emotions thickened Rosalinda's throat. This was the reason she'd chosen to be a deputy. To help people turn their life around for the better. "I wish you all the luck in the world, Daisy."

She stepped forward and gave Rosalinda a brief hug. "Thank you, Deputy Lightfoot. And if you don't mind, I'll send you a letter or card or something from time to time. Just to let you know how I'm doing."

"I'd like that very much." She looked past Daisy's shoulder. "Are you sure everything is okay right now? You need protection as you leave or anything?"

"No. It's all okay. Goodbye." She turned and hurried away, but halfway down the sidewalk, she paused and waved.

Rosalinda waved back, then watched her disappear into the darkness before she finally walked to her truck and climbed in.

Inside the cab, Rosalinda jabbed the key into the ignition, but she didn't start the engine. Instead, she sat staring out the windshield at the dimly lit sidewalk, the wooden steps that led up a grassy slope to the Blue Mesa and the planked deck where Tyler had first kissed her.

Only five weeks had passed since then, yet it felt like a lifetime. So much had happened to change her. She'd fallen deeply and irrevocably in love. But the joy of that had been fleeting. Now her heart was a broken mess, and she didn't know what to do to repair the damage she'd caused back in

Austin. Not that she'd been entirely at fault for their argument, she thought. Tyler hadn't exactly been Mr. Understanding.

That night they'd argued, he had not returned to their suite until hours later. She'd not asked him where he'd been and he'd purposely avoided any explanations. Yet even though his anger had cooled, he'd been little more than a distant stranger and they'd spent the rest of the night on separate sides of the bed.

The next morning after a stilted attempt at breakfast, they'd visited his mother one last time before catching a plane back to Lincoln County. It wasn't until they'd landed in Ruidoso and she'd attempted to tell him goodbye that he'd decided to bring up the subject of his marriage proposal. But by then, Rosalinda was so hurt and angry she'd told him that she didn't want to talk to him about anything and had walked off, leaving him standing in the waiting area.

Now, six days later, he'd not tried to contact her. And she wasn't really expecting him to. Tyler was a proud man and she supposed she'd crushed his pride. But she'd not done it intentionally. She'd only been trying to explain herself. Her feelings. And in doing so, it had come out sounding wrong and ridiculous. Now he probably didn't care if he ever saw or heard from her again.

Her eyes suddenly blurred with tears, and she wiped furiously at them before hurriedly fumbling with the key to start the engine. Yet before she could back the truck onto the street, Daisy's words were whispering through her head.

When you talked about finding the courage to make a change, I realized I had to do that. Or I would never be happy.

Dear God, it was about time she took her own advice, Rosalinda thought. She had to find the courage to trust Tyler completely. To trust that he would not only love her, but would stand up for her, protect her and stand strong when problems rained down on them. Not run out on her the way he had that night in Austin.

Quickly, she pulled back into the next empty parking spot and dug out her cell phone. Her hands shook as she scrolled through her contact numbers until she reached Tyler's. Somehow she had to convince him that she wasn't a sniveling coward. That she was brave enough to love him and be his wife.

Meanwhile, on the Pine Ridge Ranch, Tyler was going through the motions of eating supper when Gib started gathering up the dishes of food from the kitchen table.

"Did I tell you I was finished eating?" Tyler barked at him.

"You didn't have to. You haven't eaten a bite in the past ten minutes. No use in letting this stuff spoil. I didn't cook it for that."

Tyler tossed down his fork and the utensil clattered loudly against his plate. "You make me so damned mad. I don't know why I put up with you."

"Probably because you know that no one else can stand to be around you. And then you'd have to cook for yourself," Gib snapped back at him. "It's no wonder Rosa hasn't been around. You're acting like a sulking teenager."

"Don't bring her name up. I don't want to hear it."

Not bothering to look over at Tyler, Gib raked a dish of goulash into a storage container and snapped on the lid. "That's too bad, 'cause I'm gonna keep bringin' it up. You love the woman. You know you do. Whatever happened between you two in Austin can be fixed."

"I never told you that anything happened between us," Tyler countered sharply.

"Hah! Just like you needed to. You left happy, you come back miserable and Rosa hasn't been seen or heard from. I don't have to be Perry Mason to figure it out."

"Well, Perry, did you ever stop to think that seeing the

Pickens family again might be the cause of my misery, as you put it?"

"Don't try to squirm around the issue. The Pickens family has made you miserable for the past ten years. This is something else." Gib turned away from the refrigerator and pointed a knowing finger at Tyler. "As far as I'm concerned, you should be showering Rosa with flowers and diamonds and everything else you can think of. She deserves it for having the guts to face your family."

"Then why doesn't she have the guts to marry me?" Tyler burst out before he could stop the words.

Gib's brows shot up as he slowly walked over to where Tyler still sat at the table. "Did you say *marry?* You asked her to marry you?"

Tyler nodded glumly. Then, dropping his head in his hands, he said, "Gib, you understand what I went through with DeeDee. There was no pleasing her. And God knows I tried. And then when she married Trent—I felt like a failure as a man. I never thought I'd want to be a husband again. Not to any woman. But Rosa—" Lifting his head, he squared his shoulders. "Well, it turns out that I'm not man enough for her, either."

"What the hell are you talking about? She adores you."

Tyler shook his head. "That's not enough. She wants me to be some sort of gallant knight capable of slaying any dragon that tries to harm her."

Sinking into the seat opposite Tyler's, Gib asked, "Is that such a bad thing? Think about it, Ty. Rosa is clearly a strong, brave woman. Hell, she faces situations on a daily basis that would make me run and hide. But still, she's a woman. And a woman wants to know that her man will fight for her come hell or high water. That's all she wants."

What if he showed up on your ranch? He could cause all sorts of trouble for you—for us! How would you handle it?

The words that Rosalinda had flung at him back in Austin now whirled with Gib's. And suddenly everything was making sense. Rosalinda had been terrorized during her engagement to Dale. Worse than that, she'd very nearly been killed. That night in Austin when she'd been trying to explain her feelings, Tyler should have understood that deep down all Rosalinda wanted was a promise, a future with him that wouldn't crumble. And that was truly what he wanted from her, too.

"I've been acting like an ass, Gib. I'll admit it."

"Don't bother telling me what I already know. It's Rosa that needs to hear from you."

Rising to his feet, Gib patted him on the shoulder. "Use the phone in here. I'll get out and give you some privacy."

The cook had hardly gotten the words out of his mouth when the phone rang.

Tyler said, "You'd better see who that is first."

Gib picked up the receiver from the wall phone. "Pine Ridge Ranch," he answered; then after a brief pause, he turned his back to Tyler. "Yeah, he's here. No. That'll be good. Real good. Okay. Bye."

"What was that all about?" Tyler asked as Gib hung up the telephone. "If that was that damned Walt Wilson you should have told him that I already sold the horse. 'Cause I wouldn't sell him a pile of manure. He ought to be arrested for animal abuse anyway. And I—"

"It wasn't Wilson, Ty. It was Rosa. She's coming out to see you."

Stunned, Tyler slowly rose to his feet. "That was Rosa? What did she want? What did she say?"

"She was making sure that you were going to be home. I assured her you would be. That's all." Whistling a merry tune, Gib began to gather up the remaining dishes on the table.

"You go change out of those dirty clothes. And I'll make a nice dessert tray and take it to the living room."

Tyler rolled his eyes. "After the mess I made of things it'll take more than a dessert tray for me to sweeten Rosa up. But I should start calling you cupid anyway."

"You can call me cupid when Rosa changes her name to Rosalinda Pickens."

Could that ever really happen? Tyler asked himself as he hurried to his bedroom and the shower. He'd behaved badly in Austin and his conduct hadn't improved since they'd returned home. For nearly a week now he'd been nursing his crushed pride and, he was ashamed to admit, behaving like his father. When, instead, he should've been thinking of some way to prove his worthiness to the woman he loved. Now she was probably coming to tell him that everything between them was over.

But he couldn't accept that. Not ever. Rosa was his life. She and the family they could build together was all that he hoped for, all that mattered to him.

Forty minutes later, Rosa came to a stop in front of the Pine Ridge Ranch house. A light illuminated the long portico and before she could reach the steps, she saw Tyler open the door and step out to meet her.

Apparently, he had been watching for her, and her heart began to race. Was he going to tell her to turn around and leave before she even had a chance to get in the house?

"Hello, Rosa."

His deep, rich voice was like melting chocolate sliding across her tongue. Oh, how she'd missed it. Missed him. And suddenly she was thinking back to when she was waitressing at the Brown Bear Cantina so long ago. Her heart had been broken and she'd believed she'd never be able to trust anyone again. But somehow she'd found the courage to become a law officer. And then she'd met Tyler. Falling in love with him had opened her eyes and taught her so much about herself. She was a survivor and she could be anything and everything she wanted to be, including a wife and mother.

"Am I still welcome here?"

He moved over to the edge of the porch, reaching to help her up the steps. Tears flooded her eyes as she placed her fingers around his.

"Oh, Ty."

The two tiny words were all she could say, and then suddenly he was pulling her up the steps and into his arms.

"Rosa. Rosa." Burying his face against the side of hair, he clutched her tightly to him. "I'm so sorry. I've been a bastard. I should've never walked out that night at the hotel."

"No. You shouldn't have," she agreed, her voice choked with emotion. "I don't want a man that runs from me! I want one that runs to me. It's been six days, Ty, and I've not heard a word from you, much less seen you."

"I've not exactly heard from you, either," he countered. "When you wouldn't talk to me at the airport, I didn't know what to think."

Easing her head back, her gaze met his. "I'm not the only one who can get angry, and I had some thinking to do, Ty. We need to talk—about a lot of things."

"I couldn't agree more," he said, then curled his arm around her waist and urged her toward the front door. "Come on. Gib has fixed us a tray of desserts. We'll talk first, then eat."

"We're going to talk before we do *anything,*" she promised flatly.

The two of them were crossing the foyer when Rosalinda's cell phone began to ring. She paused to dig it out of her pocket.

"I'm going to turn off the sound—oh, no," she said suddenly as she noticed the call was coming from Undersheriff Donovan.

"Is something wrong?" Tyler asked quickly.

"Must be. It's Brady."

She answered it quickly and immediately her jaw dropped. "Missing? Yes, I understand. I'm here on the Pine Ridge Ranch. My weapon is in the truck. I'll leave right now. Right. Okay. Yes, he might be able to help."

Rosalinda hung up the phone. "Oh, Ty, I just said we weren't going to do anything before we talk, but it's going to have to wait. The call was an emergency. Frankie Cantrell is missing."

He frowned with confusion. "Mrs. Cantrell missing? I thought she was in Texas with her sons!"

"She was. But she came home a couple of weeks ago." Urgent now, Rosalinda grabbed him by the arm. "I'll explain everything on the way to the Chaparral. Brady thought you might volunteer to help."

He quickly turned to enter the house. "I'll get my hat and tell Gib."

Two minutes later, in her official truck, Rosalinda pushed down on the accelerator and took the turns on the graveled mountain road as fast as she could while still keeping all four tires on the ground.

As she focused on her driving, she explained the details of Frankie's disappearance to Tyler. "Brady says Frankie went out horseback riding this afternoon and never returned. Two ranch hands saw her leave the ranch and ride north. She told Leyla, Laramie's wife, that she'd only be gone for an hour or two at the most. That's all I know so far."

On the dashboard, the two-way radio continued to buzz and crackle and broken voices sounded intermittently. From earlier experience Rosalinda knew there would be no use in twisting knobs to gain a better signal. The mountains blocked out most of the radio transmission.

Tyler peered out the windshield, his gaze helping her to spot any wildlife that might be leaping out of the shadows and into the path of the truck. "Hmm. That doesn't sound like Mrs. Cantrell. I don't know her all that well, but I've talked with her a few times. Lewis, her late husband, was still alive when I first met them. She was ailing back then with her heart. A problem sort of like Mom's. But she got over it and from what Quint has told me, she's been doing quite well."

Even though the distance between the Pine Ridge Ranch house and the Chaparral was no more than five miles, it seemed double that amount to Rosalinda.

"When Hank and I spoke with her the other day, she appeared healthy and robust," she said. "But I suppose it's possible she could have suffered an incident with her heart. Or an accident with her horse. Oh, my, the family must be worried frantically."

"No doubt. And Quint's wife, Maura, is expecting their third child. This couldn't be good for her."

"Yes. That's one of the reasons Frankie returned to the Chaparral. To be with Quint and Maura while they wait for the baby. And she's concerned about all the bad things that've been happening at the ranch. I just pray she shows up soon." Rosalinda dared a glance at him. "I called the hospital yesterday and inquired about your mother's condition. The nurse said she's much improved."

"Yes. Connie took her home today." He looked at her. "I wasn't sure that you cared."

"You need to learn some things about me," she said softly. "And it looks like I need to learn them about you, too."

He reached over and touched her shoulder. "When this is over," he promised.

"Yes," she agreed while the urgency of the moment overshadowed the hope that was trying to blossom in her heart. "When this is over."

Minutes later, they found the Chaparral Ranch yard abuzz with law officers, vehicles with flashing lights, and cowboys mounted on horses and four-wheelers.

Sheriff Hamilton had set up a headquarters of sorts on the tailgate of his truck and Rosa strode through the crowd until she reached him and Undersheriff Donovan.

"We've already got a grid search started," Brady told her. "The men are slowly fanning out in a northeasterly direction. You and Tyler go drive the perimeter roads. Just in case Frankie managed to reach one of them."

"Right. Still no word or clues?" she asked before she turned to follow his orders.

He cast her a grim glance. "No. My sister is beside herself and Quint fears his mother has had a heart attack."

"I'll call in if I see anything out of the ordinary," she assured him.

She spotted Tyler waiting for her at the edge of the crowd and quickly motioned for him to join her at the truck. Once they were both in the vehicle, she said, "They've already started a grid search. Brady wants us to drive the roads. Just in case Frankie wanders onto one of them."

As she gunned the truck out of the ranch yard, Tyler said, "Hell, there's no telling how many roads crisscross this ranch. Some of the old dim trails even travel onto my property, although those are cut off by fences. Miners and hunters made them years ago. It would take us hours to drive them all."

"God willing we'll run into her before that," Rosalinda said hopefully.

"Rosa, I have a bad feeling about this. I think someone has caused Frankie to go missing."

Stunned by his observation, she eased her foot off the accelerator and looked at him. "You think she might have been kidnapped?"

"Think about it," he said. "The fire was deliberately set. Someone has been causing all those other problems for the Cantrells. Someone has Frankie. It all adds up to me."

"As much as I'd like to think you're wrong, you're making very good sense." She pushed her foot down on the gas. "I didn't ask Brady about that possibility. I suppose he and Sheriff Hamilton aren't so concerned about the why of it right now. They're concentrating on finding her."

"Yeah, but the motive might help find her."

"So where do we look?" Rosalinda asked. "It's been dark for nearly two hours now. And this ranch covers thousands of acres. If she went north, maybe we should drive in that direction. But lost people tend to go around in a circle."

"Like I said, I don't think she's lost." He stared thoughtfully out the window. "The Cantrells are worth millions. Someone might have gotten ideas to ransom her."

"Ty, if this wasn't so serious, I'd accuse you of watching too much television."

"What's a television?" he asked drolly. Then a thought suddenly struck him and he snapped his fingers. "Rosa, when you get to the next intersection, turn right. That's the road the rustlers used back when they nabbed Alexa."

"Ty, that incident has nothing to do with this and—"

"Please, Rosa. Trust me. Remember? I told you that road is not that far from my old cabin. Whoever took Frankie probably knows the area well. He or she might even think the location is too remote for the law to think of looking there."

Nodding in agreement, she said, "Okay, Ty. We're going to follow your hunch. Meanwhile, let's pray you're right."

For the next thirty minutes, Rosalinda was forced to bring the truck to a slow crawl as they steadily inched over a washed road that had gradually turned into little more than two rough ruts with waist-high grass and sage growing in the center.

When the track finally became too rough to navigate, she parked, and after strapping on her weapon, they left the vehicle and started hiking up the mountain. Thankfully, a full moon had risen and they were able to pick their way by the silvery light. But as the forest thickened, it was slow going and Rosalinda didn't let Tyler out of her reach as they climbed through rough gullies and over slabs of rock.

"An hour ago I thought this was a good idea," Rosalinda whispered between the huffs and puffs of her laboring lungs. "Now I'm wondering if we're both crazy. Why would anyone bring Frankie up here?"

"To isolate her. To avoid the law or her family. Because the person is crazy. I don't know. I'm just following the feeling in my gut."

"And I'm following you," she reminded him. "God only knows what Sheriff Hamilton might say if he knew we were up here."

"If we get Frankie back to safety he'll give you a medal,' he assured her.

Fifteen more minutes of hard climbing took them past the tiny lake and the beautiful falls. Ten more on to that brought them to within fifty yards of the cabin.

As soon as Rosalinda spotted a dim light in the tiny log house, she grabbed Ty by the shoulder and tugged him down so that they were both in a crouched position.

"Stay down!" she whispered the sharp command. "We don't want to announce our presence. Not yet."

"No one has asked me about staying in the cabin, so it's a trespasser. Or worse."

Using her head, she motioned toward the cabin. "Let's creep closer. Maybe we can hear what's going on in there."

Careful to keep from stepping on anything that would make a noise, they hunkered down and slowly picked their way to the log structure. The front door and all three windows were opened to the night air. But whoever was inside was out of view.

On the west side of the building, Rosalinda and Tyler crouched below the window and listened intently.

At first the only sound to be heard was the faint clatter of tin like an eating utensil against a granite plate or cup. Then heavy footsteps thudded close to the window, making Rosalinda and Tyler squat even lower.

Then suddenly a woman's voice spoke. "I really need to go home, Saul. I'm not feeling well. It's time for my medicine."

"Can't do that, Frankie. Not yet. I got to figure out what to do with you."

The woman sighed. "Saul, I've promised. I'll explain everything to Sheriff Hamilton. I know you're sick and not yourself. I'll tell him that I don't want charges filed against you."

"Not myself," he drawled sarcastically. "Hell, I've never felt more like myself than I do right now. I'm almost glad you found me out. At least I don't have to worry about hiding things anymore."

Rosalinda and Tyler's gazes met in the muted light filtering from the open window, and she could see he was just as shocked by the unfolding events as she was.

"Saul, you've always been a good man," Frankie continued. "When I rode up and saw you cutting that fence I could hardly believe my eyes. And then for you to pour that tainted feed on the ground, I've never been so ashamed of anyone in my life!"

Apparently, Frankie wasn't too afraid to speak her mind to the man, Rosalinda thought. Could be the woman believed she knew Saul enough to safely reason with him.

He said, "It's funny to me that you never took notice of all the good things I done around the ranch. I was just another slave to the Cantrell family."

"There isn't one person working for the Chaparral who thinks of himself as a slave. Only you," Frankie pointed out. "And I can't understand why. We've never treated you unkindly."

Saul snorted. "After Lewis died you knew I wanted to take care of you. But no, you had to take off to Texas and leave me. That's why I had to do all that bad stuff. I had to get you worried enough to come home and stay home."

His footsteps took him away from the windows to some point across the room, but Frankie's voice remained close by, telling Rosalinda that the man wasn't physically restraining her. But without looking inside there was no way of knowing if Frankie was confined by some other means.

"There was never anything like that between us, Saul. I told you that I'm still carrying Lewis in my heart. There's no room for another man in my life now."

"Well, you shouldn't have been riding your horse today. And you damned well shouldn't have ridden all the way to the flats. Then you wouldn't have caught me doing that stuff. You've messed things up, Frankie, showin' up like you did. Now I've gotta think. I gotta figure out what to do. 'Cause I ain't gonna let anybody put me in jail. No, sir."

"What are you going to do, Saul? Keep me here in this cabin forever? Kill me so that I can't talk?" Frankie bravely taunted. "That's really the way to show a woman you love her."

"Shut up! Just shut your mouth and let me figure things out or I'll throw you in that mine shaft behind the cabin and they'll never find you!"

Her mind spinning with possible solutions to get Frankie

safely out of the cabin, Rosalinda touched Tyler's hand then pointed toward the rear of the cabin.

He nodded that he understood and the two of them slipped silently to a pitch-dark spot behind the little house.

"The man is crazy!" Tyler exclaimed in a whisper so low she could hardly hear him. "We've got to get Frankie out of there!"

"I could try to call for backup, but my phone is useless up here. Besides, it would take too long. If you ask me, he's losing his grip on reality." She swiped a hand across her forehead before the balls of sweat had a chance to roll into her eyes. "It would help to know if he had a weapon. But since we don't, I'll have to go on the assumption that he does."

"You're wearing your uniform. Once he sees you he'll know his chance to escape is over. I could go in all innocent like and demand to know why he was trespassing and using my cabin," Tyler suggested. "That might distract him long enough for you to come in and get the upper hand."

She shook her head. "I don't want to risk your safety."

"Rosa, do you think I want to risk yours? We're in this together. In everything together."

She squeezed his hand, and he placed a hard, swift kiss upon her lips. In that moment Rosalinda knew that for as long as they lived, she would never doubt this man's devotion or love.

"All right," she relented. "Let's ease back to the window. When I give the signal, you make your way into the cabin. I'll be a few seconds behind you."

He nodded and they crept stealthily back to the shadowy spot beneath the window. By now the cool mountain air was growing cold with the night. If Saul was paying any attention at all, he'd soon be shutting the door and windows. They had to make their move soon.

Inside, Frankie was still bravely goading her captor.

"You're a big blowhard, Saul. And I'm going to be damned mad if something happens to my horse. Caspar doesn't know why he's tied up to a tree in the cold and the dark. He wants his oats and hay and his bed."

"That horse. That horse," Saul mimicked sarcastically. "Why don't you care about me like you do that horse of yours?"

"Maybe because Caspar is a whole lot nicer and smarter than you are."

"Why you—" Saul's words halted as something suddenly fell with a thud to the floor.

Rosalinda looked at Tyler, then made a circular motion with her finger to let him know it was time for him to move. He nodded and with her heart in her throat, she watched him disappear to the front of the house. She counted to three, then followed.

"Hey in there," Tyler called as he stepped through the open door. "What are you doing here in my cabin?"

Tyler's voice had Saul whirling around in shock. Seeing he was cornered, the man grabbed a bowie knife lying on the table.

"Get Frankie out of the way," Rosalinda shouted to Tyler. "I'll take care of him."

In the flash of an eye Rosalinda was busting Saul's arm over her knee. Once the knife went clattering to the floor, she twisted and shoved the man's elbow up to the middle of his back.

Already winded from the brief altercation, the paunchy man struggled only slightly as she brought his wrists together and clipped on the metal cuffs.

"Oh, thank God you two showed up," Frankie said as Tyler unwrapped the cord binding her hands to the chair. "I didn't know how I was going to get away from that idiot. He's the one who set the fire. The one who's been causing all the trouble."

"Yes, we heard some of what he said through the window," Rosalinda told her. "Enough to send him away for a long time to come."

Saul tried to jerk out of Rosalinda's grip, but she held him fast. "You ain't got enough evidence to convict me," he boasted. "And I ain't talkin'."

"You don't have to," Rosalinda told him. "We caught you holding Mrs. Cantrell against her will. That's kidnapping and you're going to pay dearly for it."

Rosalinda's remark clearly knocked the sass from him. His shoulders slumped and his jaw went slack. A few feet away, Tyler was helping Frankie to her feet.

"Our truck is down the mountain on the road. Do you think you can make it that far?" Tyler asked her. "We heard you telling Saul that you were feeling sick."

With a little laugh of relief, the dark-haired woman stood and hugged him tightly. "That was just a ploy. And it's downright lovely to be rescued by my neighbor. Thank you, Tyler. But I'm not going to leave this place without my horse. Will you go get him? He's tied to a tree not far from the east side of the cabin."

"What about Saul? Was he riding a horse when you came across him?" Rosalinda asked her.

"The damned nag ran off." Saul decided to speak. "He's probably back at the ranch now with his head in a feed bucket."

She nudged the old ranch hand toward the door. "All right. We'll check that out later. Get going and don't think about trying to bolt in the dark," she ordered. "I'm not averse to using my weapon if I have to."

A half hour later, Rosalinda, with Frankie next to her in the passenger seat, was driving back to the Chaparral. Saul sat in the back, cuffed to a metal ring attached to the floor of the bed, while a short distance behind the slow-moving vehicle Tyler rode Caspar. During the drive to the Chaparral, Rosalinda tried several times to radio the news that Frankie had been found safe and sound, but it wasn't until they reached the river bottom that the signal finally got through.

When they arrived at the ranch yard, a crowd of happy people were waiting for their arrival. Frankie was instantly swept up in joyous embraces from her family while Rosalinda and Tyler relayed the events that had led to the woman's rescue to Sheriff Hamilton and Undersheriff Donovan. Most of the ranch hands who'd been so diligently searching for the ranch's mistress gathered around in groups, talking in hushed tones. Clearly the men were shocked to learn that Saul had betrayed them all. And so was Hank, who'd written off Saul as being too old and lazy to be a criminal. As for Rosalinda, tonight had taught her to never assume anything until she got the facts.

"Rosa, I thought I told you to drive the perimeter roads?" Brady cocked an eyebrow at her as he waited for an explanation as to why she'd ended up so far into the mountains.

"Well, I was driving the roads," she explained. "We—uh, Tyler and I just decided to walk a ways into the woods to look around. I tried to radio. But the signal was gone."

"Conveniently so," Brady said with a sly roll of his eyes.

Tyler's arm came around Rosalinda's shoulders in a display of protective support. "I made her go to the cabin," he told Brady. "I had a gut feeling and I made her follow it."

Brady suddenly grinned at the both of them. "If you ever decide you want to go into law enforcement, Tyler, just let me know. You two are quite a pair."

Smiling, Tyler said, "I think one deputy in the family will be enough."

Brady laughed, suddenly excusing himself as someone

called to him. Tyler used the moment to pull Rosalinda away from the throng of people and into the quiet shadows of a barn.

"Tyler, did you really mean that? About one deputy in the family?"

He wrapped his arms around her. "I meant it. I'm a rancher. I don't have any desire to be a lawman. But the real question is—do you want to marry me? Back in Austin—"

"I handled your proposal badly," she interrupted. Slipping her arms around his waist, she pressed her cheek against his chest. "I realize I hurt you, Ty, and I'm sorry for that. I'm not a coward, but I must have seemed like one to you."

Groaning, he pressed his cheek to the top of her head. "Tonight proved what I already knew. You're a brave and incredibly strong woman. That night in Austin I was thinking about what I wanted instead of listening to what you were trying to tell me. Since then, I've had time to think and I've come to understand why you were afraid to say you'll marry me. So I'm making a promise to you now, Rosa. I'll never walk off again. I'll always be at your side. No matter what problems we might face in the future."

"Oh, Ty, I love you. I'll always love you. And I've been doing a lot of thinking, too. I'm a heck of a lot stronger than those old fears and I'm not about to waste any more time on them. I'll marry you tonight, darling. Tomorrow. Or as soon as we can arrange it."

Tilting her face up to his, he kissed her with such longing that tears of happiness slipped from the corners of her eyes. "Rosa, you might not believe this, but when you called earlier this evening, I was just about to reach for the phone. To call and beg you, if necessary, to take another chance on me."

She blinked at the tears that continued to spill onto her cheeks. "I've missed you so much. All this week I've been miserable and then something happened tonight—a sweet little friend helped to settle everything in my mind. Someday I'll tell you about her. But right now I think I should ask how you're going to feel about having a wife who's a deputy sheriff."

His arms tightened around her. "I'm going to feel very proud, Rosa."

"Not worried about my safety?"

"I'd be lying if I said I won't worry on occasions. But after seeing you handle Saul tonight, I know how capable you are. And I want you as the woman you are now. I don't want to change you. I've seen firsthand how that destroys people and families."

Easing her head back, she gazed up at him, her eyes shining with love. "Deputies can be wives and mothers, too. And I love my job. But I love you even more. If being a deputy ever got in the way of our marriage, I'd give it up in a flash."

"It will never come to that." He rested his forehead against hers. "Our marriage isn't going to be like my parents' marriage, Rosa. Ours is going to be an equal partnership based on love."

"Love. I'm definitely feeling that right now." She brought her lips close to his. "Do you think anyone would notice if we slipped away? Remember, Gib has made us that nice dessert tray. It's time we do a bit of celebrating."

"Mmm. From now on, every day of our lives is going to be a celebration, Rosa. So we might as well start tonight, don't you think?"

She kissed him, then with a sly little laugh, tugged him out of the shadows and toward her truck.

"Finally," she said. "The deputy gets her man."

Epilogue

November arrived in Lincoln County with a snowstorm that covered the mountains and had the skiers flocking to the area to enjoy the freshly powdered slopes on Sierra Blanca. The influx of visitors was creating extra work for the sheriff's department, but Rosalinda had managed to get the day off and she'd spent three-fourths of it riding horses around the ranch, helping her husband search for any cows or calves that might be stranded in snow drifts.

She and Tyler had been married for four months, and since then each day had been as Tyler had predicted, a celebration of their love.

"I hope Gib has something warm to drink," Rosalinda said as she kicked her boot free of the stirrup and climbed to the ground. "I think my feet are frozen. Come to think of it, my nose is numb, too. Is it still there?"

Chuckling, Tyler plucked Moonpie's reins from her hand,

then leaned over and kissed her nose. “Yep, it’s still there. Let’s get the horses settled. It’ll be suppertime soon.”

Minutes later, they entered the house, stopping by the mud room long enough to remove their coats and hats before moving on to the kitchen. Inside the blissfully warm room, Gib was at the stove stirring something that smelled like chili. Nearby, Edie Pickens stood at the cabinet counter tearing lettuce into a wooden bowl.

“Do I need to get out the ice pick and chip the icicles off you two?” Gib asked.

“How about a blowtorch?” Rosalinda joked as she flexed her stiff fingers.

“Mmm. I smell something spicy and warm,” Tyler said. “How long until supper?”

“Not long,” Gib answered. “Edie has cornbread baking in the oven. It’ll be done soon.”

As soon as Edie had gotten well and back on her feet, she’d shocked everyone by filing divorce papers. The ranch patriarch had initially exploded, but once he’d seen that Edie wasn’t going to back down, he’d realized that his marriage was over. Edie hadn’t asked for much in the divorce settlement; her freedom had been her real reward.

Tyler had been just as surprised as everyone else about his mother’s change of heart. Because he’d experienced firsthand the terrible results of meddling in someone else’s marriage, he’d never urged Edie to divorce the man. And though he wanted his mother to be happy, Rosalinda understood there was a small part of him that hurt because his parents were no longer a loving couple. But then, he’d be the first to admit that they’d not been a loving couple for many years. The divorce had only legalized the situation.

For the past month, Edie had been living with them on the Pine Ridge Ranch, and during that time Rosalinda had watched a frail, timid woman blossom into a stronger, happier person and the bond between her and her mother-in-law was growing stronger every day.

Walking over to his mother, Tyler put his arm around her slender shoulders. "Mom, are you telling me that Gib is actually letting you help him cook?"

Edie laughed. "Gib knows he doesn't have to worry about me taking his job."

Gib chuckled. "Well, I'm sure not opposed to having help. In fact, I'm downright enjoying it."

The smiles on the two men's faces reminded Rosalinda of just how much their lives had changed since that day she'd arrived here on the ranch to question them about the fire. The big house was a home now, with rooms full of love and laughter.

She only wished that things were going so well with Tyler's family back in Texas. During the past couple of months, Tyler and Warren had exchanged a few phone calls. Clearly, there was still a huge gulf between the two men, but at least they were both trying to communicate with each other. And that was a start at rebuilding a bridge between them.

However, the situation with Trent wasn't as hopeful. His drinking had steadily worsened and Warren had seemingly lost any chance of redeeming his son. For reasons that appeared to be purely financial, DeeDee had decided she didn't want a divorce after all and was doing her best to lure Trent back home. Tyler wanted no part of his brother's life. Not until the other man decided he wanted to live in a decent, worthwhile manner.

As for Rosalinda's family, she and Tyler had traveled up to Gallop for a visit and the Lightfoots had all promised to come to the ranch over the holidays. She was very much looking forward to a big family gathering.

Walking over to the patio door, Rosalinda peered out at the snow-blanketed ranch yard. "So what do you think about this snow, Edie?"

"It's beautiful," her mother-in-law answered. "It makes me think Christmas is coming."

"It is coming, Mom," Tyler spoke up, then looked to Rosalinda and smiled. "And we're going to have a big party. Rosalinda's family is coming and we need to invite the Cantrells and some of the Chaparral hands, along with all the Pine Ridge cowboys. Don't you agree, honey?"

"Oh, yes," Rosalinda agreed, her eyes shining. "It'll be such fun. With a big tree and twinkling lights and all sorts of good food."

"Friends and family," Tyler mused aloud. "That's what Christmas is all about."

Rosalinda couldn't help but notice that Edie's expression had taken on a forlorn look.

"It sounds wonderful," the woman said wistfully. "We've not had anything like that on the Rocking P since you twins were little boys. I wish I could be here."

Hurrying over to the woman, Rosalinda asked, "Why can't you be here, Edie? Don't you like it here with us?"

Tyler's mother gave her a wobbly smile. "I've never been so happy," she admitted. "But you two are still newlyweds. You don't need your mother-in-law around, getting in the way, taking away your privacy. I've already out-stayed my welcome. I'm going to have to find a place of my own in Ruidoso or somewhere nearby."

"Don't talk that way," Rosalinda gently scolded her. "This house is enormous. When Tyler and I want to be alone, we can find a spot."

Tyler chuckled. "That's right. We can go all the way to the old cabin if we have to," he teased, then seeing the uncertain look on his mother's face, he gently touched her cheek. "Mom, seriously, we'd love to have you here for as long as you want. But if you want to have a place of your own, that's your choice. That's the most important thing. And it's the one thing Dad never gave you."

"No," she admitted. "I never got to have a say about anything at any time. Until you and Rosa gave me the strength to do something about it."

"Well?" Tyler prompted. "Are you going to hang around and help Gib chase after all the babies Rosa and I are planning on having?"

She looked at Rosalinda, then to her son, and suddenly her eyes filled with happy tears. "I wouldn't miss that for the world."

"Amen," Gib exclaimed. "Now get the cornbread out of the oven, woman. It's time to eat."

Later that evening, after the hearty meal, Rosalinda and Tyler sat snuggled together on the couch while they gazed at the low-burning flames on the hearth.

"Mmm, this is nice. Just you and me and the glow of the fire," Rosalinda murmured.

He pressed a kiss to her temple. "You've been so generous and loving to welcome Mom into our home. Thank you for that, my darling."

A drowsy smile tilted Rosalinda's lips. "We're all family, Ty, and we'll be even more of a family when our first baby arrives."

Twisting around, he stared at her with hopeful excitement. "Are you trying to tell me you're pregnant?"

She cupped her hand to his lean cheek. "Not yet. Are you disappointed?"

With a sexy chuckle, he pulled her onto his lap and brought

his lips down to her. “No. It gives us reason to try again. And again. And again.”

Her soft laugh was smothered by his kiss.

* * * * *

It turns out someone else has a secret on the Chaparral—
Sassy!
Keep an eye out for the next Special Edition
Men of the West title from
Stella Bagwell!

When a dangerous storm hits Rust Creek Falls, Montana, local rancher Collin Traub rides to the rescue of stranded schoolteacher Willa Christensen. One night might just change their entire lives....

***

"Hey." It was his turn to bump her shoulder with his. "What are friends for?"

She looked up and into his eyes, all earnest and hopeful suddenly. "We are, aren't we? Friends, I mean."

He wanted to kiss her. But he knew that would be a very bad idea. "You want to be my friend, Willa?" His voice sounded a little rough, a little too hungry.

But she didn't look away. "I do, yes. Very much."

That pinch in his chest got even tighter. It was a good feeling, really. In a scary sort of way. "Well, all right, then. Friends." He offered his hand. It seemed the thing to do.

Her lower lip quivered a little as she took it. Her palm was smooth and cool in his. He never wanted to let go. "You better watch it," she warned. "I'll start thinking that you're a really nice guy."

"I'm not." He kept catching himself staring at that mouth of hers. It looked so soft. Wide. Full. He said, "I'm wild and undisciplined. I have an attitude and I'll never settle down. Ask anyone. Ask my own mother. She'll give you an earful."

"Are you trying to scare me, Collin Traub? Because it's not working."

He took his hand back. Safer that way. "Never say I didn't warn you."

She gave him a look from the corner of her eye. "I'm onto you. You're a good guy."

"See? Now I've got you fooled."

"No, you don't. And I'm glad that we're friends. Just be straight with me and we'll get along fine."

"I am being straight." Well, more or less. He didn't really want to be her friend. Or at least, not *only* her friend. But sometimes a man never got what he wanted. He understood that, always had.

Sweet Willa Christensen was not for the likes of him….

***

Enjoy a sneak peek at USA TODAY *bestselling author Christine Rimmer's new Harlequin® Special Edition® story, MAROONED WITH THE MAVERICK, the first book in* MONTANA MAVERICKS: RUST CREEK COWBOYS, *a brand-new six-book continuity launching in July 2013!*

HSEEXP0613

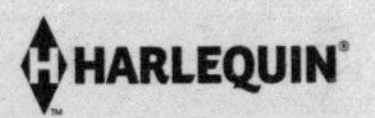

SPECIAL EDITION

Life, Love and Family

Be sure to check out the last book in this year's Mercy Medical Montana miniseries by award-winning author Teresa Southwick.

Architect Ellie Hart and building contractor Alex McKnight have every intention of avoiding personal entanglements while working together. However, circumstances conspire to throw them together and the result is a sizzling chemistry that threatens to boil over!

Look for Ellie and Alex's story next month from Harlequin® Special Edition® wherever books and ebooks are sold!

HARLEQUIN®
A Romance FOR EVERY MOOD™